"We're compatib___ __ ___ her hot cheek to ___ Her skin leapt at the caress. "We get along well enough. We both love Molly. We could make it work."

He reached up and smoothed Lea's hair from her damp face, his eyes appealing. "Molly could have a proper brother or sister and the baby could have a full-time mother."

She stared, wide-eyed, trying not to savor the feel of his fingers on her face.

"Be open to all the possibilities, Lea. Just think about it."

Her voice was no more than a whisper. "You want a family that much?"

"As much as you did five years ago."

She slipped her hand to her belly to protect the innocent life within. *Her child.* The planet's gravity seemed to shift and cause a delirious weightlessness in her. It was the perfect solution.

And the absolute worst.

"What about love?" she whispered.

OUTBACK
Baby Tales

Newborns, new arrivals, newlyweds

In a beautiful but isolated landscape, three sisters follow three very different routes to parenthood against all odds and find love with brooding men.

Discover the soft side of these rugged Outback cattlemen as they win over these feisty women and a handful of adorable babies!

NIKKI LOGAN
Their Newborn Gift

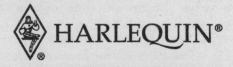

TORONTO • NEW YORK • LONDON
AMSTERDAM • PARIS • SYDNEY • HAMBURG
STOCKHOLM • ATHENS • TOKYO • MILAN • MADRID
PRAGUE • WARSAW • BUDAPEST • AUCKLAND

Recycling programs
for this product may
not exist in your area.

ISBN-13: 978-0-373-17664-9

THEIR NEWBORN GIFT

First North American Publication 2010.

Copyright © 2010 by Nikki Logan.

Nikki Logan lives next to a string of protected wetlands in Western Australia, with her long-suffering partner and a menagerie of furred, feathered and scaly mates. She studied film and theater at university, and worked for years in advertising and film distribution before finally settling down in the wildlife industry. Her romance with nature goes way back, and she considers her life charmed, given she works with wildlife by day and writes fiction by night—the perfect way to combine her two loves. Nikki believes that the passion and risk of falling in love are perfectly mirrored in the danger and beauty of wild places. Every romance she writes contains an element of nature, and if readers catch a waft of rich earth or the spray of wild ocean between the pages she knows her job is done.

Visit Nikki at her Web site, www.nikkilogan.com.au.

For Cadel

Who fought hard to get to us and who is brilliant,
living proof of the value of IVF.

Thanks to Michelle and Melissa, who were such a
pleasure to share this series with and who were so
generous and welcoming to the new girl.

To Kim Young, for your confidence in my stories.

Lastly, with thanks and admiration for all the people
who have worked so hard to save the extraordinary
Kimberley region from feral predators, only to have
bulldozers flatten it to make factories.
Keep fighting the good fight, folks.

Start your Kimberley journey here:
www.kimberleyaustralia.com.

CHAPTER ONE

'OH, YOU are such a cheater…'

Lea Curran swiped at the tears in her eyes, convinced she was going to run off the gravel road any second. *Cause of death? Laughter.*

Amazing she could still laugh at all, really.

She trained her eyes on her daughter's face in the rear-view mirror. 'Since when does Boab start with a T?'

'T for tree.' Four-year-old Molly giggled. It set off the usual heart-squeeze in Lea. Her giggles gave way to full tummy-laughs and then to heaving, hacking coughs. Lea's smile stayed glued to her face through sheer will-power. She watched her daughter in the mirror for any sign that her distress was more than usual. But Molly—amazing Molly—just let the spasms pass, recovered her breath and went right on playing their driving game.

As though every kid in the world coughed when they laughed.

'Your turn, Mum.'

Lea shifted her eyes back to the road. 'I spy, with my little eye…'

Their game went on as bush scrub whipped past the car, kilometre after kilometre.

Molly's body might have been falling apart, but her four-year-old brain was as sharp as ever. She compensated for her extremely limited physical stamina with a relentless intelligence that certainly didn't come from the Curran side of the family. She could play this game for hours. They'd been on the road for three.

Molly finally identified Lea's 'W' word—wing mirror— and looked expectantly at her mother for more.

'I spy…' Lea's chest clenched as she looked ahead '…something beginning with M.'

Her sharp little daughter didn't miss a beat. 'Mum?'

'Nope.'

'Molly?'

God, she loved her! 'Outside the car.'

'Oh.' Mini eyebrows scrunched down over serious brown eyes then shot up. She didn't notice their vehicle slowing. 'Monkey?'

'We're in the Kimberley, Molly, no monkeys here. Good try, though.' Lea glanced at the turn-off ahead and swallowed hard. A giant sign marked the turn-off for the Martin property.

'Min…am…' Molly read the giant red letters as best she could.

'Minamurra,' Lea assisted, turning the wheel and taking the car under the arched sign. Even she could hear the flat lifelessness in her voice as she added, 'You win.'

'Is that where we're going?'

'Nope.' Lea swallowed hard. 'It's where we are.'

Molly must have caught some of her mother's trepidation, because she would usually have laughed at Lea's corny joke. She sat higher in her booster seat and peered out of the window, gnawing on her lip—one-hundred percent from her mother, that little habit—then her eyes refocussed and her pale lips split in one of her blindingly heart-stopping smiles.

One-hundred percent her father's.

'Horses!' She pointed to where a dozen working-horses grazed peacefully in a paddock. The eucalypts lining the long drive whizzed by, making the pastoral scene look like an old flicker-film from the thirties.

Molly disappeared back into that place she went to when she was in a particularly happy mood, when she wasn't too sapped. Right now, she was talking about the horses with the invisible sisters she took with her everywhere. Imaginary Annas and Sapphies of her own.

Lea forced her focus off the mirror and up towards the house emerging through the eucalypts. The homestead seemed to grow towards them like something from a nightmare. Large, expensive and looming.

Her fingers started to tremble on the steering wheel.

A house like that had to have a family in it. It had no wife, as far as she'd found out, but maybe a girlfriend. Parents.

More obstacles. More people to judge her. More strangers for Molly.

She guided her car over a sequence of cattle grids into Minamurra's lush heart. Beautiful gardens offset the trappings of a working station: heavy equipment, sheds, stables, beat up four-wheel drives. They must have tapped straight into the aquifer to have this kind of green in the middle of a Kimberley dry season. She pulled to a halt in the shade of two towering kurrajongs standing like sentinels at the base of old timber steps that cut up through the turfed knoll leading to the house. She left the engine and air-con running, and crossed to Molly's door.

As she cut around the front of the car, her eyes slid sideways and followed the long steps upwards just in time to see a tall figure emerging from the house onto the veranda, sliding a hat onto his head and staring curiously in their direction.

Lea held her breath.

Reilly Martin.

The last time she'd seen him he'd been sprawled naked across the motel bed in a deep, exhausted sleep as she'd snuck out into the dawn like a thief. Pretty apt, as it turned out.

She bent down and kissed Molly through the open window and asked her to sit tight for a bit.

Not only was Reilly not expecting anyone, he definitely wasn't expecting anyone with legs like that. What was she doing—trying to climb in the back seat through the window? It looked like the car was trying to swallow her.

Or was she just trying to make a memorable first impression? She wouldn't be the first woman to drive all the way out here to try her luck: a waste of their fuel and his time.

He had nothing to offer them. Not these days. They came expecting Reilly Martin the national champion. King of the Suicide Ride. They left cursing him and kicking up dust in their haste to be gone. The in-between had grown too predictable. Too painful.

If this one turned around with suitcases in her hand, he would go back inside and lock the door. Bush code be damned.

She turned.

No suitcases. His spine prickled and he squinted against the afternoon sun, trying to place her as her coltish legs carried her up the steps towards him. There was something about her. The higher she climbed, the more backlit she was by the sun blazing fiery and low in a deep-blue west Australian sky, until she was the best part of a rose-edged silhouette. Quite literally the best part. With her T-shirt tucked into her jeans, she was pure hourglass, and she moved towards him like one of his best mares.

This was no circuit-chaser.

'Hey,' the silhouette said softly.

Only his dirt-crusted boots stopped him from flinching backwards from the hoof to the belly that was her voice. One word, one syllable, from the apparition approaching and he knew in an instant. The soft voice was burned into his memory, like his diamond-M marked the flesh of Minamurra's horses.

It was her.

It was hard to forget the woman who'd made you feel as cheap as a motel television.

It had started as sex—a typical, sweaty, body-rush circuit encounter—but it hadn't ended that way. Not for him. There'd been something so raw about her. She'd been almost frantic at first, and he'd had to gentle her like a skittish brumby, using his voice, his body, his strength.

It wasn't until she'd looked up at him with those old-soul eyes that he'd realised just how lost she was. The look from the bar. Like a fish that knew it was miles from its nearest water, but was determined to stay on dry land even if it killed it.

The look had intrigued the heck out of him.

After that, she'd swung right into the spirit of things. Admirably. It had been a long, memorable nineteen hours holed up in that motel. He'd never in his life been so ensnared by a woman, by her body, by her quiet, empty conversation, by the *something* that had called to him in the bar. It had been the first and only time he was a no-show for an event. But dropping his place on the ticket had been worth it.

She'd been worth it.

And then he'd woken up to an empty bed and her share of the room rental lying on top of the TV. No phone number, no forwarding address, not even a 'sorry' note. No matter how many trophies he had, how many newspaper clippings, how many fans, she'd been a painful reminder of what he was really worth.

He shoved his hands into his pockets. That was hardly about to change now.

His heart hammered against his moleskin shirt as she paused on the top step.

'Do you know who I am?' The same nervous quality, underlain with a huskiness that took him straight back five years to that room.

Like he could forget. But he wasn't giving her that much. He tipped his akubra up and squinted at her, swallowing carefully past a dry tongue. 'Sure. Lisa, right?'

She stepped forward into the shade of the veranda and he caught the tail end of an angry flush. 'Lea.'

'Sorry. It's been a while. How've you been?' Dropping back into casual circuit-banter came all too easily. He'd learned early how to make conversation with strangers; it was a survival tool in his family: meaningless, empty conversation while your guts twisted in on themselves.

Her breath puffed out of her. 'Is there somewhere private we can talk?'

Apparently, the lovely Lea wasn't as gifted in the 'meaningless chat' department. He followed her glance back to the tinted glass of her car. A haze of emissions issued from her exhaust. He frowned. Was she so eager to be gone that she'd left her motor running? He finally noticed how sallow she was beneath the residual blush. Almost green, in fact.

That, combined with the getaway car, finally got his attention.

He looked at her seriously. 'We can talk right here. There's no one in the house.'

'I... Your parents?'

'Don't live here.' Why would the beautiful people choose to hang out in the depths of outback Western Australia? Visit, absolutely. Live and die here, nope. That was fine with him.

'A, um, girlfriend?'

His eyes dropped to her lips briefly. 'No.'

She glanced around at the stables and yards. 'Station hands?'

'What do you want, Lea?'

Her back straightened more than was good for a spine.

Sorry, princess; a few great hours do not entitle you to a thing.

Okay, a night. And part of a day.

She glanced back at that damned car. 'I... It's about that weekend.' She cleared her throat. 'I need to talk to you about it.'

Despite her obvious nerves, he felt like needling her. It was the least he could do. 'It's five years too late for an apology.'

The flush bled away entirely. 'Apology?'

He leaned on the nearest veranda-post, far more casually than he felt. 'For running out on me.'

Her colour returned in a rush. 'We picked each other up in a bar, Reilly. I didn't realise that entitled either of us to any niceties.'

Oh, yeah, he much preferred her angry. It put a glint in her eye only two degrees from the passionate one he remembered. 'How did you find me?'

The anger turned wary. 'You were the talk of the town that weekend. I heard your name somewhere, remembered it. I looked you up in the championship records.'

Her enormous pupils said she was lying. Why? Damn her, that he still gave a toss.

'Which brings us full circle.' He straightened so he could glare down at her. 'What do you want, Lea?' he asked again.

She blew out a breath through stiff lips and turned to walk a few paces away. 'There's something about that night—something you should know.'

Understanding hit him like a hammer blow. 'You told me you were clean.'

She stumbled to a halt. 'What?'

'You told me you were clean and on birth control. It's why we didn't use more protection.'

That felt like a critically stupid decision now. But somewhere in the back of his thumping head, a rational voice told him he hadn't caught anything off this woman. It would have shown up in one of the multitude of tests he'd undertaken since then— pure luck, considering how dumb it was to have had unprotected sex. But his big brain hadn't been doing the thinking that night.

Her eyes flared. 'I am clean. I'm not here to tell you I've given you something.'

'Then what the—?'

'I came away with something that night.'

What? 'Not from me, lady.'

She hissed. 'Yes, Reilly. From you.'

'Are you the man with the horse?'

The little voice threw him. He and Lea spun round at the same time and she dropped instantly to her haunches before a tiny, dark elf standing at the top of the steps. The elf's brown fringe was cut off square across her forehead, and her hair fell down straight on either side of her too-pale face. She seriously looked like something from a storybook. Not in a good way.

'Molly, I told you to stay in the car.' Lea pushed the girl's fringe back from her forehead and laid a hand against her skin. 'Did you climb all these stairs?'

It was only then he noticed the kid was wheezing. Badly.

She wriggled free of her mother's fussing and looked straight at Reilly with enormous, chocolate-brown eyes. 'Can I see it?'

Somewhere deep in his gut a vortex cracked open. He knew those eyes. His pulse began to hammer but he managed to keep his voice light even as he towered over the tiny girl. 'See what?'

The kid looked to Lea and then back at him, her dark brows collapsing inwards. 'Mum said she needed to see a man about a horse.' She sucked her lip in between her teeth. 'I wanted to meet the horse.' A spasm of coughs interrupted her wheezing.

Lea slipped her fingers around to the girl's pulse, concern etched on her face. She threw him a desperate look.

He stepped closer then put the brakes on. Not his problem. 'Is she okay? Does she need a drink of water or something?'

'Please.'

Reilly was only too happy to get away from the surreal scene for a moment. His thumping head now echoed through his whole body. He let the screen door bang shut behind him, knowing he could see out better than she could see in, and he turned to watch the woman and child framed in the doorway.

Lea was older than when he'd last seen her, but it only showed in the worry lines marking her hazel eyes. The rest of her was still as long and lean as when they'd first met. She loosened the little girl's shirt, pushed sweaty hair back off her face and then lifted her into her arms. Two tiny sticks slid effortlessly around Lea's neck, and mother and daughter had a low, private conversation punctuated with soft, loving kisses.

It was so foreign. Yet he couldn't take his eyes off them.

I came away with something that night. His blood chilled. Not possible. Just not possible.

Five years ago, a frozen inner voice reminded him. *Very possible.*

Little Molly tilted her head and rested it on her mother's shoulder, staring straight down the hallway, where he knew she couldn't see him through the tinted mesh.

He recognised that face. It was in the one photo he had kept of himself as a child.

Oh, God...

A black hole opened up in his gut, and a million possibilities rushed in right behind it. Possibilities he'd thought lost to him for ever. He kept his heart rate under control by pouring two glasses of ice-cold water in the kitchen, and then he shakily tossed one back himself before steeling himself to return. Mother and daughter whipped around as the screen door opened, and he indicated the comfortable cane-seating further along the veranda. She lowered Molly into a chair. It dwarfed her, her little legs stuck straight out in front.

More sticks.

'Thank you.' Lea's voice was as unsteady as the hands that took the water from him. She gently placed the other one out of reach. 'Molly can't be near glass.'

Reilly frowned. Lea tipped her own water up to Molly's bloodless lips. The girl gulped greedily, then Lea drank from the glass herself, visibly mastering her breathing. Max, his house cat, chose that moment to appear and twist himself amongst Lea's feet. She leapt six inches off the timber floor.

It was not a discussion to have in front of a child, but he had to know—right now. 'Is she mine, Lea?'

Lea's head snapped up, her eyes wide, fearful.

'Kitty!' Molly's delighted squeal broke the silence. Reilly snagged Max up off the ground and dumped him unceremoniously in Molly's chair. The girl fell on him with open arms. Max looked suitably disgusted.

Lea's mouth opened to protest, but then she snapped it shut.

'What—she can't be near cats either?' Shock was giving way to sarcastic fury.

Lea shot to her feet and spoke to Molly. 'You play with the kitty, sweetheart.' She crossed to the far corner of the veranda. Reilly followed.

'She's mine, isn't she?' He loomed over her intentionally. He wanted the truth from her almost as much as he wanted to smell her. Lea nodded and his chest constricted, bright light exploding behind his eyes. His mind worked furiously.

'Did you not think I'd care?' he asked. Lea turned away from him. 'Did you think I'd tell you to get lost?'

'I wasn't looking for a relationship,' she whispered back over her shoulder. 'I saw no need for you to know.'

'No need?' She winced and he struggled to keep the edge out of his voice. He knew what impact it had on his toughened workmen; Lea was not one of them. 'I got you pregnant, Lea. I would have stood by you. By Molly.'

No matter what the world expected of him, he would have done that much.

She spun. '*I* got me pregnant, Reilly. There was no need for

you to stand by me. I was fine. I made the decision to go ahead
with the pregnancy. It didn't need a team.'

There was something in her tone, like the particular look in
a stallion's eye when he was about to turn. It screamed a
warning at him. Suspicion stained his words. 'I can't believe it
took you five years to find me.'

Her furtive glance told him it hadn't. *Ah.* 'You weren't going
to tell me.'

Her chest heaved. 'No.'

'Nice.' He meant her to hear his mumble.

'Don't you judge me, Reilly Martin,' she snapped furiously.
'If you cared so much where your DNA ended up, you wouldn't
have distributed it so liberally across the district.'

Slap! Being true didn't make it any less pleasant to hear. He
could have little Mollies scattered across the state.

In theory; he'd loved and left enough women.

Anger boiled up furiously between them. 'Did you think I
was a good catch, Lea?' He nearly spat the words at her. How
stupid had he been to think *he* had been the reason they'd gone
so long and so hard that weekend? To think that she might have
felt the same indefinable connection he had, despite running out
on him. 'The heir to a country-western fortune. Had you been
tracking the circuit long waiting to bump into me?'

'I didn't plan it! I might have made some bad choices five
years ago, but that wasn't one of them.'

'You didn't know who I was?' He let the challenge roll out
like giant rolls of straw shoved off the back of a feed truck. Her
hesitation gave her away.

Blush-heat raced along her cheekbone. 'Everyone knew
who you were, Reilly. You'd just brought home the rodeo
champion's cup. You were Reilly Martin, king of the Suicide
Ride. I practically had to join a queue.'

For what good it had done him. 'I'm sure the challenge
made me all the more attractive.'

Lea's eyes flamed. 'You don't really need much help with
that, Reilly. I'm sure you're not going to tell me I was the first
bar-room pick-up you'd ever pulled?'

Self-loathing added its weight to the discussion. 'Not by a country mile, sweetheart.'

The blush doubled. It intensified the glitter in her eyes, and did unhelpful things to his resolve. He dropped his face from her gaze. 'I'm not the point of discussion here. You are. Or rather, Molly is.' He met Lea's eyes again. 'You cheated me out of knowing my daughter.'

Damn, that felt weird, coming out of his mouth.

Lea paled and her eyes widened. She struggled against something internal. 'No one forced you to have sex with me. Fatherhood is a risk you were taking every time you went with any woman.'

'Particularly a deceitful, immoral one.'

Pain streaked across her face. She sucked it up, took a deep breath. 'Look, it happens, Reilly. Birth control fails. It's why they print warnings on the boxes. You could have walked away first that night.'

No. Not if he'd tried.

They glared warily at each other, like a cattle dog and a steer sizing each other up. 'Why me, Lea—of every man in that pub?'

Her eyes rounded—not the question she was expecting, obviously—but she pushed her shoulders back and answered. 'You stood out for two reasons. You were—'

'Male and stupid?'

Her eyes hardened. 'Attractive but unhappy.'

An ugly laugh cracked through his lips. 'Unhappy? I'd just won the champion's cup, I was surrounded by women and was working my way through a keg of celebratory beer. Why would I be sad?'

If she noticed how he'd remembered so much about that night five years ago, she didn't comment. Lucky; it would be tough to explain.

She barrelled on, ignoring the question. 'I'd had... I wasn't feeling the best that night.' Something in her expression told him there was a heck of a lot more to that story. 'And there was something in your eyes that I recognised. Some pain that spoke to me.'

He snorted to cover up how close to the mark she suddenly

was. No way was he going there. 'I'm guessing my inheritance probably spoke to you loudest. Is it speaking to you now?'

She gasped. Her nostrils flared and she tossed her thick hair back. 'Have I asked you for money?'

'I'm sure you're getting round to it.'

'I'm not here for that.'

'Then why are you here? Why now, Lea, five years into my daughter's life?' There was that word again. It was going to take some getting used to.

Deep shadows crossed her eyes. 'Believe me, I wouldn't be here at all if I had a choice,' she blazed up at him. 'We were doing just fine, Molly and me.'

Were? His eyes drifted to the little girl, who had Max in a delighted stranglehold. The cat swished his tail impatiently but knew better than to lash out.

Lea took a deep breath. 'My daughter's dying, Reilly.'

Reilly staggered backwards, and his eyes fell on the little piece of innocence tangled around his cat. He'd only discovered her moments ago. Then Lea played a particularly stinking card.

'*Our* daughter's dying,' she continued, her voice dead and tight. 'She has aplastic anaemia; it's a disease of her bone marrow. I'm not a tissue match.'

He turned back to her tortured face, his mind buzzing. 'You want to know if I'm a match?'

She shook her head. 'Even if you were, the success of adult-to-child transfer is too low.'

He ran stiff fingers through his hair. 'I don't understand. What do you want from me?'

She took a deep breath and locked her hazel eyes onto his. He'd never encountered anything quite as beautiful as the loving determination burning there. For a split second, he wished it burned there for him. When had anyone looked at him like that? Ever?

The silence screamed. And then she spoke.

'I need you to get me pregnant again so we can save Molly.'

Lea had never seen someone shrink like that right before her eyes. Reilly sagged back against the timber posts enclosing the veranda.

'Molly's dying?'

Well, at least he was focussing on the most important part. 'Gradually.' Her voice cracked and she swallowed hard. 'Yes.'

He looked at her. 'Is she in pain?'

Her heart softened. Very definitely the most important part. Finding he was still capable of the compassion and kindness she remembered was a relief. He hadn't shown much of it until just then. 'Not always. But she's exhausted perpetually, and she bleeds very easily.' And four-year-olds were prone to tumbling over all the time.

He nodded, digesting. 'And having a second child will help her—how?'

Lea was prepared for this question. 'Cord blood. And placenta. The baby wouldn't be touched at all.' She threw that in hastily, knowing it was what she'd want to know in his position.

'Stem cells?'

Lea nodded. His eyes swam with uncertainty. His breath came heavily. Then he pinned her with his gaze. 'How does it work?'

Lea lightened like helium. Was he considering it? She rushed to answer, knowing this stuff back to front. 'Cord-blood stem cells can become almost any other type of cell in the body, whatever needs repairing—bone, tissue, muscle. Marrow, in Molly's case. She can grow healthy marrow. She can make healthy blood.'

'Don't they have banks for cord blood now?'

Lea clamped down her frustration. Did he not think *she'd* thought of those things? Her child's life had been worth an exploration into every medical possibility. And every moral one. But she held her temper, moderated her breath.

'The genetic mix of people from regional north-west Australia is too specific—part-indigenous, part-Asian islander, part-European. There's nothing like that gene mix sitting in cord-blood banks around the world.'

'What about a cousin or something?'

Another deep breath. Sapphie had already offered her new baby's cord. Anna's infertility was none of his business. 'Not closely related enough. This treatment requires the cells to be from a full sibling.'

He tipped anguished eyes up to her. 'A second baby could have the same condition.'

Lea shook her head. 'It's not genetic.'

He considered that. 'A baby conceived with an agenda?'

Lea laughed, an ugly, angry sound. 'Believe it or not, this is the best available chance Molly has. Please, Reilly; I know it's unconventional, and I know I am probably the last person in the world you would want to help, but I'm not asking for me. I'm asking for that little girl.' They turned to watch Molly leap off the chair and limp after Max along the veranda. '*Your* little girl.'

Reilly swung an angry gaze back to her. 'Now that it suits you.'

She deserved that. '*Any* little girl, then. Your body produces billions of cures for Molly in a week. I just need one. Just one, Reilly.' She grabbed at his shirt, willing to beg if that was what it took. Anything for Molly. 'To save a child's life.'

She watched the anguish turn to anger. Disgust leached out at her and he pulled away from her. 'Let me see if I understand this—you tricked me out of one child, and now you're trying to emotionally blackmail me into fathering another one?'

'No. This is not blackmail.'

'Really? "Give me a child or this one dies"—what would you call it?'

She sucked in a wounded breath. 'The last act of a desperate woman! I didn't have to tell you, Reilly. I could have just arranged to bump into you somewhere, sweet-talked you into a repeat performance for old time's sake.'

He snorted. 'You overestimate your charms, Lea.'

She knew she deserved the pain that lanced through her. Her voice dropped to a whisper. 'I wanted to be honest this time. I couldn't do it that way again.'

'Why not? You applied yourself so diligently to the task last time. Or have you forgotten?'

Never. He'd been so gentle that night, as she had fallen apart from grief in his arms, grief from losing the father she'd never been able to love. Grief enough to make her do something entirely out of character while the rest of her family had been off burying him.

She might have shoved it far down into her subconscious, but no; she'd never forgotten that afternoon. 'I've lived with that decision for five years, knowing it was the wrong thing to do. Knowing I should have told you.'

'You didn't exactly rush to rectify it.'

She dropped her eyes and cleared her thick throat. 'I was ashamed. I thought…'

'What?'

She looked over at her baby. 'Maybe Molly is sick because of me. Because of the lie I told, every day I didn't tell you about her.'

All the anger drained from his handsome face. 'You don't seriously believe that?'

'I believe in a whole bunch of things I never used to.' She dragged her eyes up to his and hated herself for the tears that started to fill them. 'But this is *my* price to pay, not Molly's. She's barely started on life.'

Indecision skittered across his face, and something else: a deep sadness. 'There must be some other way to help her.'

As if she hadn't exhausted every possible alternative before debasing herself before the man she never thought she'd see again. Before exposing her shame. 'Do you think I'd be here now if there was *any* other possible way?'

His bitter laugh physically hurt. 'I know you wouldn't.'

But he hadn't had her escorted from the premises. Maybe there was hope yet. He cast his focus out over his vast property, hid his thoughts. Then his eyes returned, a fork of brown hair falling into his eyes as he shook his head. 'To make a child just to save a child…'

'What—seems wrong to you? You've been a father for three minutes, Reilly. I've lived with that little girl for five years. Carried her, then held her for over four years. Nothing is too great an ask.'

'But a baby…'

'I would love this child just as much as Molly. And she'd adore a brother or a sister to grow up with.' Instead of having to create imaginary ones.

'It just seems…' He looked over at Molly.

Lea grabbed his sleeve desperately. 'They throw them away, Reilly. They toss twenty millilitres of precious, life-saving stem cells into an incinerator once the baby is born and the cord is clamped—the cells that could save Molly. How is *that* right?'

His brown eyes smouldered like coals as he considered her. It pained her to see disgust in eyes so like her daughter's.

After an age, he spoke. 'I'm sorry Lea. I can't help you.'

She staggered back, speechless. She'd been prepared for a humiliating, difficult battle, but in her wildest imaginings she'd never thought he'd simply say no. Not the man she remembered. The man whose eyes had plagued her dreams for two years until she'd finally banished him.

'You won't help?' His lashes dropped. Lea gripped his shirt-front with both hands. 'You don't have to do a thing. You'll never even see us again. There's no expense, no obligation, I promise. Just the…' She couldn't bring herself to say 'conception.' 'We've done it before. Please, Reilly. *Please.*'

'Lea.' He took her icy hands in his and backed her to the side of the house. 'You barely know me, so I'll forgive your assumption that I would willingly impregnate you with a spare-parts baby and then walk away from any child of mine. But you aren't hearing me.'

His jaw was rigid. 'I can't help you, Lea. I can't give you a sibling for Molly.' He twisted her clenched fingers away from his body. 'You'll have to find another way.'

CHAPTER TWO

THERE were no other ways.

The reality of that had sunk in well and truly overnight, after she and Molly had returned home to Yurraji. The poor kid was crashed out in bed, exhausted from the excitement of an all day road-trip, her exertions climbing Reilly's stairs and then running around after his cat. That was all it took these days. It was now morning and Molly had slept through from sunset the night before. It was the kind of sleep Lea could only dream of.

The sleep of the dead.

Lea's eyes filled with tears. It seemed impossible that she had any left at all after a night of silent sobbing. Reilly had been her best and her last hope.

And he'd said no.

The sheer injustice burned like battery acid in her gut. That a stranger could decide whether her daughter lived or died, and that he'd done so in a matter of moments. She twisted her entwined fingers until they ached.

She'd already called Dr Koek and broken the bad news, and her specialist had immediately gone into super-supportive, damage-control mode, citing statistics to show that cord blood from an unrelated, unmatched baby could work.

Statistically.

Maybe.

Lea let her head drop to the railing surrounding her house paddock. She would try unrelated cord blood—of course she would, as many times as the specialists would allow—but something deep down inside her told her it wasn't going to work. This was the price she would pay—Molly would pay—for her past mistake.

Her sisters would pray to God and the universe, respectively, but Lea begged karma: *please,* please *do not make my baby pay for something I did. Punish me.*

Punish *me.*

A small mob of grazing kangaroos in the next paddock stood tall and looked east to the highway.

In the same moment, Lea realised there was no greater punishment for a mother than to watch her daughter die. And then live a long, miserable life with that knowledge. Her stomach heaved.

The roos lurched into flight, springing away and covering the large paddock in a few easy bounds. Lea frowned and turned in the direction they'd been looking. She saw the advancing plume of red dust drifting up over the kurrajongs long before she heard the engine.

Moments later, a battered Land Rover picked its way down her rocky drive. She recognised it instantly and her gut lurched. The last thing she'd done before roaring out of Minamurra's beautiful heart, right past this very vehicle, was to hurl a scrap of paper with her phone number and address at Reilly. She'd had no expectation that he would use it, and certainly not within fourteen hours. Not given the disgusted, pained expression on his face when she'd finally bundled up Molly and left.

Why was he here? She refused to let herself hope. He'd been brutally clear yesterday afternoon. She hardened her heart in anticipation of his next attack.

He parked his vehicle then loped towards her, looking as fresh as if he'd just stepped out of a shower, not driving since before dawn. Her mind whizzed back five years to the memory of him stepping out of the motel bathroom, unashamed and glorious. She forced herself to remember the man he really was.

'Lea.'

'Something you forgot to say?' *Some organ you forgot to rip out and pulverise under your boot?*

His eyes flicked over her shoulder, looking at the horses grazing in the paddock behind her. Then they slid back to hers. 'I came to see if you were all right.' He must have realised how utterly ridiculous that sounded, and he hurried on. 'And to explain. In case I wasn't clear.'

She straightened against the cool of the morning; it wouldn't stay that way for long. It would be forty Celsius by mid-morning. 'You were perfectly clear. You won't help Molly. I get it.'

He sighed. 'Not won't, Lea. *Can't.*'

A sleepless night and complete emotional collapse had left her preciously short of patience. 'Philosophical objections, I presume?' she snapped. She'd been prepared for that; stem cells were a touchy subject all round. The only people she'd got absolute acceptance from were her specialist and her sisters.

His jaw flexed. 'Physiological objections.'

Lea frowned.

'Saying you took me by surprise yesterday is an understatement,' he went on. 'I was completely pole-axed. I wasn't thinking straight. I should have stopped you when you took off—explained.'

He looked uncomfortable. Critically so. His eyes darkened a shade. 'I was diagnosed two years ago. It has a long medical name, but the short version is that I sustained a string of groin injuries riding the broncos over the years, and my immune system kicked in to protect itself from the damage. But the antibodies didn't only battle the infection.'

A cold chill crept through her. Lea knew all about the immune system from studying Molly's condition.

'The antibodies attack my sperm as though they're foreign objects.' He took an enormous breath. 'I'm sterile, Lea.'

The dramatic way he paled as the word crossed his lips told Lea it was the first time he'd said it out aloud. Her mind spun. 'But Molly?'

'The specialists weren't able to estimate how long ago it started.'

Not five years ago, evidently.

Sterile. Her first thought should have been for her daughter.

Saying no because you couldn't, or because you wouldn't, was still a 'no'. The 'why' made little difference to Molly.

But all the difference in the world to Reilly.

She thought about the man with the sexy swagger she'd met in the pub and tried to imagine him sterile. She remembered his potent, muscular body arching, taut, over hers and tried to imagine it barren. She looked at him now, really looked, at the extra lines in his skin, the caution in his manner, the shadow behind his eyes.

Double horror hit her. For Molly and for Reilly. That such a vibrant, virile man should be robbed of the chance to make children, the most fundamental biological right. He'd had tragedy in his life too.

'I'm sorry, Reilly.'

He pushed past to walk towards the horses. 'I'm not interested in your pity; I simply wanted you to understand my position.'

As if she could have missed it. Lea closed her eyes. She'd exposed Molly, brought this man back into her life, for nothing. He was powerless to help.

Her voice was as quiet as the morning. 'I understand.'

'What will you do?'

She shook her head. 'We'll try regular cord blood. Hope. Pray.' Her voice cracked on that word.

'That won't work?'

Lea sighed, tight and small. It hurt her chest. 'I don't think so, no. But it's something.'

Reilly stared hard at her. 'She's a great kid.'

It almost killed her to deliver a flat smile. 'She is. The best.'

She stepped up to the paddock fence as one of her horses walked over. As always, she drew comfort from Goff's softness and courage from his warmth. She could feel Reilly's eyes on her through the silence. He stepped closer behind her.

'Lea, if there was…' He seemed uncertain; it didn't suit him. He cleared his throat. 'If there was a way despite my…'

Lea's radar began to bleep. But, no, she'd felt like this walking up his stairs, and look how that had worked out. She forced down the little spike of hope, turned to him with a purposefully bland expression.

His eyes raked over her, wondering, worrying. 'I told myself I wanted nothing to do with you. Even for Molly,' he said. 'But I lay there last night thinking about this little pixie of a kid and how she looks just like me at her age. And I realised I couldn't do *nothing*. She's my daughter. My blood. I spent most of the night online researching her condition.'

His tanbark eyes burned with intensity and he shook his head with disbelief. 'I didn't tell you about my situation so you could feel sorry for me. That's the last thing I want. But you need to understand this is not a small thing you're asking. Quite apart from the philosophical considerations, as you so aptly put it, I just don't have millions of cells to work with. You're not asking for something minor.'

That made it sound like... Her heart started to thud.

He broke a long silence. 'When investigations first began, one of my many medicos recommended freezing a sample for later comparison, assuming we'd have something later to compare with. They used most of it up running a fortune's worth of tests.'

Lea's breath evaporated. *Most.*

He turned and looked at her. 'But there is a freezer in a lab in Perth and it contains one single remaining sample, about the size of one of Molly's fingernails.'

Lea's heart lurched to a halt.

'If it's like the others, it won't have a lot in it, but it may just have enough. Enough to help Molly.' He stared at her in silence while her mouth opened and shut like a baby barramundi.

Words simply would not come, trapped behind a lump the size of a football in her throat. She had a sudden flash of a teenaged Molly—healthy and happy, her whole life ahead of her—cantering a greying Goff around the paddock. And Reilly, the man with only one shot at fatherhood, who was willing to spend it on a daughter he'd only just discovered. A daughter whose parentage he'd not even asked for hard proof of, so strong was his instinctive recognition that she was his.

Lea pushed up onto her toes and threw her arms around Reilly's surprised neck. For a moment, the very barest of moments, his arms crept around her and a fluttering sense of rightness ghosted through her. But then his hands slid upwards, gripped her shoulders and pushed her firmly away, his eyes locking onto hers. She felt instantly cold.

'I'm doing this for Molly. Not for you. I have no interest in helping you beyond what it does for my daughter.'

She ignored the hurt snapping at her heels like a cattle dog, accustomed to forcing down personal pain. Her vision blurred with tears. 'I understand.'

'And it's not without a price. There's something I want in return.'

'Anything.'

His dark eyes glittered. 'Careful, you don't know what I'm asking yet.'

There wasn't a single possibility she hadn't thought about before driving to Minamurra, a compromise she wasn't willing to make. She'd already given him her body, albeit in a moment of grief-stricken insanity. There was nothing he could ask that she wasn't ready to grant. For Molly.

She tossed her head back and met his gaze head-on. 'What do you want?'

'First, I want to be able to see Molly regularly. I want to be part of her life.'

Lea took a deep breath. Since he was the one saving Molly's life, that wasn't unexpected. She would watch him like a hawk until she could determine whether he was a man like her father…or something else.

She nodded slowly. 'Agreed.'

Reilly looked at her, his dark gaze unfathomable, probing, intense. The hairs on Lea's neck stood to attention and her skin tingled.

'And second…'

Here it comes. He was going to ask her for a physical commitment. A tiny part of her wasn't dreading it. She remembered every moment from five years ago and the primal haven that was his embrace.

'…I want custody of the child we make together.'

Gravity suddenly altered its fundamental principles. Lea would have gone down if not for Reilly's iron grip on her upper arm.

'Given the sacrifice I'm making, it seems a reasonable trade,' he said. 'You get Molly's cordblood, I get an heir.'

CHAPTER THREE

LEA'S skin prickled despite the morning heat. To find hope only to have it ripped violently away again... Her hands shook. Her voice was strained.

'No.'

'Lea, think about—'

'No!' She marched off toward her house, heart thumping painfully. She needed to be close to Molly right now. Badly. How could he think, even for a moment, that she would... could...? Her chest tightened like a slingshot. She spun round, wounded beyond measure that he thought that of her. 'You cannot ask that. It's not fair.'

'How fair was it to rob me of a child? To bring her to me only when you needed something?'

'I had no choice!'

'Neither do I, Lea. You're handing me a miracle. How can I just shrug that off?' He pursued her across the house-paddock, snagged her arm and spun her back round to him. 'I remember something you said when we were together, about how disconnected you felt from the world.'

'I said way too much that weekend.' Her determination to keep her distance had lasted all of an hour. After that first sweet time together, she'd opened up to him like he was her confessor, believing she'd never see him again.

'I don't have to tell you about loneliness, Lea. Surely you can understand why your request might be like a beacon in the darkness? The chance I believed I'd never have?'

Lea's chest lifted and fell with her tumbling thoughts. Of course she could understand it. Molly had been her own beacon, even the very idea of Molly. It was why it had been so easy for her subconscious to subvert her morals five years ago and keep the pregnancy a secret. Her father had done such a prize job on her trust in men—in anyone—she'd given up any hope of meeting someone to have a child with. To have one simply gifted to her... It had felt very fated. Divine.

Was that how he was feeling? *Damn him.* 'Reilly, you're asking me to give you my child.'

'And you're asking me to give you *mine.*'

Lea blinked furiously, realising for the first time just how much she was asking. Her mind worked frantically to find escape. 'Do you have any idea how to be a father? How will you possibly raise a child alone?'

'You managed.' He rushed on as Lea opened her mouth. 'And, before you play the "I'm a woman" card, ask yourself whether you'd accept that if you were in my position.'

Lea's mouth snapped shut with a click of teeth.

He stepped closer. 'I'm granting you the last of my sperm. What you need to save Molly. I understand the price is high but so are the stakes for me.'

She stared at him through watery eyes. 'It's more than high. I can't do it.'

Reilly stiffened his back. 'Then I'll fight you for Molly.'

'No!' The fierce yell practically tore its way out of her constricted throat.

Reilly stood his ground and pointed at her heaving chest. 'There, Lea. Take those feelings you're only barely managing to suppress and multiply them by one hundred. That's how you're going to feel if you walk away from this chance—Molly's last chance—and she dies.'

It was all too easy to imagine how that day would feel. She thought about it every day. Lea's whole body shook. Months of suppressed agony, of having to be strong for Molly while fearing the worst, hit her full in the chest. She nearly crumpled.

Nearly. At the last second she swayed back into a surer

position. Her voice was thick and strained. 'There must be some other way.'

His hoarse laugh grated on already tattered nerves. 'Sure—you could marry me and raise the baby together.'

She smiled tightly at him. 'I'll pass, thank you. When I said you were my last choice, I meant it.'

His lips thinned. 'What happened to you doing whatever it takes to save Molly?'

'You can't tell me that's your preference?' she gaped.

'Tie myself to a woman who lied and cheated me out of a child? Who only surfaces when she wants something, and who asks me to be a stud-bull?' His contempt was palpable. 'You even need to ask?'

Silence. Goff snorted in his paddock.

Finally Reilly spoke. 'I've told you what I want, the terms under which I'm prepared to help Molly.'

Lea's snarl was heartfelt. 'What sort of a man sets terms on saving his daughter's life?'

Brown eyes blazed. 'A desperate one.'

Lea clung to the doorframe and watched Molly sleep. Tired as she still was, she slumbered deep and long, her breathing shallow, her skin almost translucent. Surrounded by her toys, she looked for all the world like she was laid out in state.

Macabre but at peace.

Few days were peaceful for Molly, and they were getting fewer. She'd gone far beyond benefiting from treatment; it was now essentially for survival. Without the stem cells, Molly wouldn't live to go to school.

What Reilly was asking was effectively blackmail. To put such a condition on the life of a child. It was why she'd thrown him and his selfish needs off her property, sent him packing back to Minamurra.

What sort of a man wouldn't give up even the last of his sperm to save a dying child?

A desperate one, he'd said.

Not so desperate he hadn't thought the finer details through and laid it all out for Lea as she'd stared, horrified, at him. She would carry the baby to term and doctors could harvest the umbilical stem cells. Then she and Molly would head back to Yurraji, and the baby would be packed off with a nice big tin of formula to the home of a man with no wife who knew nothing about rearing children. He didn't even have brothers and sisters to have learned from.

It meant nothing that she'd seen a softer side to him five years ago, a side that had potential to grow into the sort of patience and compassion required in a parent. She'd seen not a hint of that today. Or yesterday. The new Reilly Martin was one-hundred percent diamond-ore; cold, hard and unmoveable.

She shook her head. This was the man she'd let into Molly's life. Molly she could at least buffer, but she couldn't protect a new child, living alone three hours away with a monster.

Reilly's minimal interactions with Molly flashed through her mind like a reluctant slideshow—how instinctively gentle he'd been with her. Okay, so he wasn't likely to be a total monster, but still—what kind of man would make such a request?

What kind of woman would? It was true she was asking him to give up a child.

But in all her planning and visualisation it had never occurred to her he would *care* about the baby that would result, let alone want it. The paradigm she was working from was five years out of date: Reilly Martin, king of the circuit; lover of women; drinker of beer.

Wanter of heirs, apparently.

She shuddered in a breath. If anything happened to Lea, Molly would go to Reilly. She'd created that reality the moment she'd driven down Minamurra's long, tree-lined drive. Never mind that her will named Anna and Jared as Molly's guardians; Reilly would not rest until his daughter was with him. His threat to fight for Molly might only have been a ploy to win an argument, but if Lea wasn't around to intervene, her daughter would grow up a Martin.

Then again, without this particular Martin, her daughter wouldn't grow up at all.

The dark, ugly thought crept through and brought her back to Reilly's request. To give him the baby when it was born; it would virtually be surrogacy. The incubation of a child that wouldn't be hers, never mind that biologically it was. She'd considered doing it for Anna and Jared, but her sister wouldn't hear of it, wouldn't put someone she loved through the pain of surrendering a child.

What Reilly was proposing would be just the same, except she'd be taking her payment in the form of stem cells, more priceless than any money.

But giving up the baby…

Molly's eyes began to shift beneath her lashes. The anxious twitching of her fingers meant it was more nightmare than dream. Lea crossed to sink down onto Molly's bed and placed her hand gently on her daughter's chest, speaking quietly to her. The twitching ceased immediately. A moment later her damp brown eyes fluttered open wide. She stretched up for a big hug and clung hard to Lea's neck. Lea kissed her and kept up the reassuring murmurs.

'Where were you, Mummy?' Molly's breathless little voice asked. Even hugging her mother made her puff. Lea held tighter.

'I was right here, chicken.'

Her little face frowned with confused concentration as she fell back onto her pillow. 'You were gone. I was alone.'

Lea smoothed Molly's fringe back from her eyes. 'Shh. No. I was here. I'm always going to be here, baby. You were dreaming.'

'It was nice there. But I was alone. Don't leave me alone, Mummy…'

Lea dug her fingernail into her thumb hard to channel the pain, to focus the grief, not to think about the symbolism of Molly's dream. It took everything she had not to let the tears well up and spill over in front of her anxious daughter. Time enough for that later.

'Do you feel like waking up now?' Lea's voice was painfully tight. Molly rubbed dark, deep eyes and shook her head.

'Okay. How 'bout I sit with you here until you go back to sleep and I'll make sure you don't go back to the place where you were alone—okay?'

''Kay.' Molly sucked her thumb into her mouth and then rolled onto her side. Lea tucked her in more firmly and gently rubbed her back until she felt her daughter's breathing regulate. Then it was safe to let the tears creep out. They streamed, unchecked, down her face accompanied by the silent sobs she'd become so adept at.

Minutes passed and Lea's whole body hurt from keeping the pain inside. She sucked in deep, shuddering breaths then tiptoed out of Molly's room and headed for her mobile. She punched in Reilly's mobile-phone number and pecked out a concise text-message with badly shaking fingers.

Just three words: *I'll do it*.

CHAPTER FOUR

THE conception of their second child was a far cry from their first. Even Reilly appreciated the irony.

Three weeks of blood tests, injections, headaches and hormones, until Lea's body artificially ripened to bursting point, followed by scans every three days until her eggs were perfect for harvesting. Then the city specialist who had been flown in accessed Reilly's tiny, frozen sample and injected the healthiest thaw survivor directly into one of Lea's eggs.

Shame had been a near-permanent resident in Reilly's throat, knowing there'd been barely any sperm left, the rest biologically massacred by his over-zealous immune system.

Now, Lea stared rigidly at the beige ceiling and did her best to ignore him and the six people in the room all fussing around the business end of her body where her legs were braced in stirrups and her hospital gown was tented over her bent knees. As if she needed the privacy from herself.

Reilly's gut tightened and his temperature raised. He hadn't realised how humiliating this would be for her when he'd insisted on being present for the implantation. Or that every muscle in her body would tremble uncontrollably. Empathy washed through him.

They'd tried to convince him it was nothing they hadn't all seen before, but the excited buzz and the number of personnel present seemed to indicate an ICSI implantation was something several of them had very definitely not seen before in their remote hospital posting. He could see the bright lights, the graceless position, the room full of strangers, were all starting to get to her. Even with sedation slowly kicking in.

His lips tightened. Could they make this any more uncomfortable for her?

Molly might not have been conceived in love, but at least it had been natural, the joining of two people who had connected for a preciously short time. In a bed. With sweat. This man-made artifice was so foreign.

But entirely appropriate under the circumstances.

Lea sighed, just when he might have himself. He glanced back at her eyes and saw they were getting more glazed as the sedation continued to take effect.

'Lift your hips slightly, Lea? Good girl, thank you,' the specialist requested from down near her feet. She flinched at something being done down there. Three pairs of eyes glanced up at her over blue hospital-masks, then at the clock on the wall. Was she taking too long to relax?

'Why are all the blue people talking so loudly?'

At least he thought that was what she said. Her speech reminded him of the lost tourist they had found out on the far corners of Minamurra one time, half-frozen after a night in dry, sub-zero Kimberley temperatures.

Lea started to fight the sedation and he took her hands to stop her waving them about. She forced her head towards him, as though he were a life buoy in a tossing sea, and stared at him with vulnerable, anxious eyes. A pang bit deep in his chest. 'You're okay, Lea.'

'Reilly?' Her frown doubled even as her hand-hold grew tighter.

He turned to the nearest doctor. 'Should she be in this much distress?'

The doctor rested his hand on her calf kindly. 'She's not really responding to the sedation as we would have hoped.'

Lea Curran doing something completely contrary to the norm? No surprises there.

'We've ceased the feed now. It'll ease off shortly.' The

doctor's attention went back under the sheet as yet another man in blue bustled in the door and dived under the screening covers at the foot of the bed.

'Jeez, buy a girl a drink first,' Lea said, over-loudly, then started to giggle. Not in a good way.

Reilly stood. 'Okay—essential personnel, stay. Everyone else, out.' He was counting on everyone in the room assuming he was the loving husband, that he had a right to issue orders on Lea's behalf. Apparently they did. Half the room left with baleful glares, only the chief doctor and two nursing attendants staying. Both of them kept a respectful distance.

At last.

Lea didn't look at him but he was sure he heard her voice thank him.

The tiny whisper made him inexplicably tight-chested. If he hadn't bullied his way in here, she would have been doing this completely alone. Where the blazes were her sisters? Had she even told them this was happening? What kind of a crazy family did she come from, anyway? Just when he thought families didn't come worse than his own.

He shook his head. Neither the Currans or the Martins could be stranger than the family he and Lea were in the midst of making—one child conceived by accident, a second through negotiation, despite him having vowed all his life never to replicate the mistakes of his past.

The child they were making today might grow up motherless, but there were worse things. Like growing up with a mother who created a child for what it could give her, rather than to bring a life into the world for its own sake.

A mother like his own.

Lea mumbled incoherently and Reilly forced his gaze back to her. Motives aside, this woman had brought him the miracle of fatherhood, not once, but twice. Long after he'd given up all hope of ever experiencing it. For that, she deserved his tolerance, if not his friendship. He might not like her values very much, but Lea Curran had unintentionally given him the biggest gift of his life. Two children.

The doctor caught his eye and nodded. Reilly leaned in close to Lea's ear and tightened his hand on hers. 'They're going to start now. Are you ready?'

Her glazed eyes met his and she nodded, just before her lashes slipped down to rest on her cheeks.

'Wake up, Lea, you'll want to see this.'

He risked a gentle stroke on her flushed cheek, just below where her lashes lay like freshly cut grass. She curled her face into his fingers and he gently ran his knuckles across her perfect skin, memory surging back. God help him if she remembered this later. 'Open your eyes, Lea. Look at our baby.'

The word 'baby' brought her focus hurtling back, as though she'd suddenly realised what was happening. That she was being implanted, right now, and that the last man in the world she would want watching was here, holding her hand.

He let his hand drop with the pretence of taking her chin and turning her face towards the large-screen monitor. Every eye in the room was fixed on that screen, and the blurry shapes on it suddenly started to make sense to both of them.

Lea's eyes widened as far as his. 'That's my uterus.'

He couldn't help the heat that leached up his throat. There was something so intensely personal about looking at a woman's womb. Fortunately, all eyes were on the screen, where a long, thin curette delivered the sole viable embryo into its thick, warm bosom of flesh.

'Oh, my God.' Lea said it. Or maybe he had. Her fingers found their way to his again.

A tiny dark mass trembled on the end of the glass straw for two heartbeats and then broke free, like an astronaut launching weightlessly into space, suspended in the jelly-like delivery medium. Reilly's eye locked onto that dark mass as the curette withdrew. His throat tightened up.

The specialist straightened. 'All finished. Well done, Lea.'

From the corner of his eye he saw Lea glance up at him, and watched him staring at the tiny speck on-screen. 'It's amazing,' he mumbled, and then his eyes dropped to hers and rested there a moment. This was as close as he'd been to her for five years. Since he'd warmed her naked body with his own. His heart kicked up a beat or two.

Her hand still held his in a death grip. She opened her mouth to say something.

'How do you feel, Lea?' The specialist appeared behind him and peered at her. Reilly slipped his hand free and moved back out of the way, letting the specialist in to question his patient. He saw her try to follow him with her eyes but he moved faster than her groggy head would allow.

Outside Theatre, he sank into the nearest empty seat, as buoyant as if he'd actually seen his child being born. He held a strange new glow close to his heart. This baby would know the sweet touch of its father's unconditional love, not grow up as an accessory to its sister. He would raise it to love the country as much as he did, and eventually to take over Minamurra.

He blew out a controlled breath and wondered what his parents would say when they discovered their barren son was the father of not one but two children. Why did he feel like not telling them at all? He shook his head against the crazy urge to hand out cigars. Cigars were for celebrations, and this was hardly an event he'd want anyone congratulating him on.

He'd just created a life to save a life.

Built a baby.

It was a fraud.

And he knew all too much about that. In Reilly's case, his own conception had been a double fraud. His mother had got pregnant back in the last weeks of the crazy seventies when her career as half of the country-western act Martin and Lynnd was looking shaky. The public scandal of her pregnancy had assured her place in the spotlight, and the fact that the father was her long-time singing partner had ensured a fast marriage and secure future.

Adele Lynnd was nothing if not goal-oriented.

Reilly had come along just as the wedding gifts had started to run out of warranty and the publicity had dropped off. A series of family spreads in popular magazines had ensured public attention peaked again. There was only one photograph of him as a child—the only one he still had, from an avenue other than a media photographer. Lucky he had been such a good-looking baby. Then again, as the articles said, how could he not be with such a gloriously handsome mother?

Reilly frowned. For most of his childhood, he had felt the sting of being an inconvenience, an irritation, but on those rare occasions when something he'd done had delighted his mother, he'd been gifted the full brilliance of her attention and her spectacular smile. It had worked on a young Reilly every bit as well as it had worked on the people of Australia.

No wonder he'd grown to be such an over-achiever.

It had been tough enough to explain walking away from the circuit at the top of his game to the reigning monarchs of country music. But telling them their trophy child wouldn't be making any trophy grandchildren any time soon…

Not pretty.

Their reaction had reinforced his belief that he'd lost the one virtue he could have added to this stinking planet. The one thing that set him apart from every other ringer out there scrabbling for the handful of women prepared to live in the bush. The only thing that had made him a prospect for netting a good outback woman to grow old with: his top-grade, celebrity-issue, prize-winning Martin DNA.

If he'd been a stallion, they would have shot him. On the worst days, he wished they had.

'Mr Martin?' A passing nurse dropped her mask and gave him a pretty, sexy smile. He recognised the speculative sparkle of someone who was interested, and he frowned. For all she knew, the love of his life was next door being impregnated while she was out here flirting with him. The disrespect rankled.

Even though it was only Lea.

The smile dropped away as she read his disapproval. 'Ms Curran is asking for you. She's nearly ready to go.'

Reilly straightened immediately. Asking for him? He struggled to imagine it. Then again, she'd clung to his hand earlier like it was the only thing keeping her here on Earth. Even through the distraction of what he'd watched happening, he'd been conscious that, the last time she'd gripped his entwined fingers like that, they'd been pressing into a motel mattress.

He tried not to go back there any more, not to cloud what should be a business arrangement, regardless of how he'd held those memories in the past.

Now she was asking for him. He hurried ahead of the nurse back into the room, inexplicably moved by the expectant hope in Lea's rapidly clearing gaze.

'Reilly.' She peered at him bright-eyed as he sank down next to her. 'How's Molly?'

Molly. Why had he expected different? He tried not to be jealous of a sick four-year-old child simply because her mother's world began and ended with her. Wasn't that how it was supposed to be? Wasn't that how love worked in normal families? But it didn't make him feel any less like he was only valued—once again—for what he could provide, rather than who he was.

Was his life destined to repeat itself for ever?

Lea didn't need the pregnancy test to tell her Reilly's embryo had taken, but she'd done it anyway. She couldn't wait the extra few days before her results come back from the city; it had been hard enough to wait the obligatory two weeks.

She pressed her warm cheek to the cool tile of the bathroom wall and groaned. She'd forgotten this part—the soul-destroying nausea. It had started almost immediately when Molly had been conceived too. It was how she'd finally realised she was harbouring a tiny life. She closed her eyes and breathed deeply.

She slid her trembling hand around to her warm belly as if the tiny being in there could turn off the sickness at will. At least she got to do this privately, for two more weeks anyway, until Reilly's first access visit. Lord knew there was precious little about this pregnancy she would experience by herself. Between her sisters' over-enthusiastic involvement, the doctors' very clinical interest and Reilly's presumptions, there were barely any secrets left.

Her satellite phone rang. She glanced at it with suspicion.

Surely Anna wouldn't ring back so soon, not after Lea had prac-tically hung up on her to go and lose her breakfast? She frowned. Maybe Anna had set Sapphie onto her. It wouldn't be the first time her two sisters had teamed up like cattle dogs to muster her in one particular direction: theirs. They wanted to know whether there was going to be a new Curran in the family.

Lea sagged against the wall. There wouldn't be, even if she was pregnant. But she hadn't told them that. Some small part of her was counting on the fact that she had nine months to think of a solution.

The phone rang on. She ignored it. Even her gorgeous half-sister was beyond her today. Sapphie deliriously in love was twice as exhausting as Sapphie on a regular day. There was only so much sunshine and flowers a girl could take when her body was rejecting its own stomach-lining.

And if it was someone else on the phone? Ha. Who else would it be? Someone from Parker Ridge? She could count on one hand the number of people who'd rung her in nearly six years at Yurraji.

'Mad horse woman.' 'City conservationist.' 'Bloody nuisance.' She'd been called it all. Now they could add 'single mother of two' to the list of her apparent social-crimes. She didn't care what people two hours away said about her. The only thing she cared about was Molly and twenty precious millilitres of stem cells.

She let the phone ring out. It rang again almost immediately. *Oh, for crying out loud!* She jagged the phone up with the opposite hand to the one holding the home-test stick and barked a curt greeting. 'What?'

'Are we pregnant?'

Reilly was intimidating even without being in the room. Something about the way his voice rumbled across the phone line started a tremor spidering down her back. It had been like that when he'd first spoken to her in that pub. When he'd slid all six-foot-plus of himself into the shabby seat opposite her and refreshed the Chardonnay she'd been nursing all afternoon.

He'd spoken exactly as he looked: sexy as anything.

In her grief it had been easy to talk herself into it. Who would it hurt if she connected with someone just that once? Someone tall. Broad. Solid.

Someone alive.

Life, as it had turned out, was dangerously short. As her father had learned.

She stared at the tiny white stick in her hand. 'We'll know in ninety seconds.'

'Do we just sit here in silence?' He sounded testy across three hundred kilometres.

Despite her churning stomach, Lea smiled. So, Mr. Smooth was capable of getting ruffled. Good to know. 'What would you like to talk about?'

'What if you're not pregnant?'

'They've held a tiny fraction of your sample over. We try again.'

Reilly's convoluted contract allowed for that. The legal documents were necessary, and not unexpected, but were still a slap in the face, a reminder that this was pure business to him. But after a second attempt there would be no sample left. No contract. No Molly. Lea straightened. 'But there's no reason it won't take. It was six days old, and quite robust by embryo standards, apparently.'

She fought to keep the hint of pride out of her voice. She had no business feeling proud about this baby. In fact, she'd do better not to think of it as a baby at all, knowing she had to hand it over to Reilly. It was an umbilical cord, that was all.

Its job was to attach to her.

If she grew attached to *it* she'd never be able to fulfil the terms of Reilly's agreement.

'We haven't yet locked down the timeline for my visits.'

Lea rubbed her temples. No, they hadn't. She wasn't sure she wanted him visiting Yurraji every four weeks. But it could have been much worse. 'Will you come to us each month?'

'Unless Molly would like to break it up a bit—see Minamurra occasionally?'

'We'll see.' A dull thud started up behind her left eye. She'd grown so used to only worrying about the needs of her daughter and herself. Driving out to Reilly's property would be doable, except in the final few weeks of her pregnancy.

Assuming she got pregnant at all from the implantation. Her eye went back to the stick. Nothing yet.

'How is Molly?'

'Molly's…' *Not having the best week.* She'd spent a lot of time in bed this week, pale and unhappy. It only shored up Lea's resolve to get this new baby safely born. But there was no need to share her worry. 'Sleepyhead is still in bed.'

'Does she know I'm coming next week?'

'End of next week.' *And not a moment sooner, thank you very much.* 'She does. She asks after you all the time.' Unpalatable, but true.

Reilly considered that in silence. 'Thank you for telling me.'

'You thought I wouldn't?'

'It wouldn't surprise me.'

Because I'm such a liar and a cheat. Lea knew she deserved some of Reilly's anger, but not all of it. He'd been a willing participant that day five years ago. *She'd* been hypnotised by the local celebrity and district hottie with eyes straight out of a cologne advertisement.

What was *his* excuse?

'I have no interest in robbing Molly of her father,' she whispered.

Now. She almost heard him thinking it down the phone. 'You told her I'm her father?'

'No. Not while she's so little. But I told her you were going to be the new baby's father and you might like to be her daddy too.' She cringed at how intimate that sounded.

'A daddy that doesn't live with you?'

'Molly and I have been alone for so long, she doesn't know any different. It's going to be years yet before other people start making her doubt herself.'

A raven cawed outside Lea's window. Reilly's voice dropped a note. 'Is that experience talking?'

She was not going to discuss her father with him. How she'd wished for most of her life to be free of Bryce Curran and his dodgy values. Fate had handed her the most tangible kind of freedom five years ago and she'd fallen entirely to pieces. She'd staggered to her car amid the suddenly booming silence at Yurraji and started driving in a daze. She hadn't stopped until she'd found a town filled with strangers and rodeo competitors.

She'd left at dawn, just as bemused. And pregnant, as it had turned out. Her eyes dropped now to the hand clutching the damp stick and she felt the room rush around her like a whirlpool. She sucked in a deep breath. And another.

'Lea?'

She glanced across the living room to where Molly's bedroom door stood ajar so that she could see her exhausted little figure twisted around the two-million stuffed toys that shared her bed. Her eyes fluttered shut.

Thank you.

'Lea? Are you still there?' Genuine concern saturated his words.

'Sorry, I'm here. I'm just…' She took a deep breath, and looked at the little stick. 'Pregnant.'

CHAPTER FIVE

GETTING Reilly to wait until his access weekend took a lot of negotiating on Lea's part. He'd wanted to come immediately on hearing the little stick was showing positive. What was he going to do, come over and stare at her non-existent belly for six hours? Lea's fast talking had finally persuaded him to achieve as much as he could over the following few days so he could clear his schedule and spend a full day with Molly on his access day.

He'd shuffled his schedule around and left his station hands in charge of running Minamurra. Anyone else might have taken the opportunity to talk up how much work went into breeding and training the district's finest working and endurance horses and how indispensible he was, but Reilly had simply shrugged and said, 'I pay them well to make sure I'm expendable.'

Now Lea's heart squeezed as she looked down her house-paddock to where Reilly and Molly stood discussing the two workhorses, Pan and Goff. The smaller horse lazed his way over to the fence as the humans approached—breakfast, he probably figured—and Reilly reached out and scruffed Goff's mane high between his ears. The gelding ate it up, tipping his head in for more.

Traitor.

Molly imitated her father, stretching her little leg up to brace one foot on the first rung of the timber fence, resting back on her hip and folding her arms on the timber paling above it. On Molly, it looked adorable. On Reilly…

Lea turned away from the compelling portrait. They were nearly an hour into Reilly's first visit and no disasters yet. That didn't mean it wasn't going to be the longest of days.

'Mum,' Molly called from the fence line, her eyes saucer-sized. 'Reilly's going to let me ride Goff!'

Lea's whole body stiffened. Her mouth dried and she sputtered, furious at Reilly for suggesting such a stupid thing, and angry at herself for not taking him through the rules more thoroughly before he'd even set foot on Yurraji. She'd counted on him exhibiting *some* common sense.

'Molly, honey.' She crouched as her daughter skipped over, uncharacteristically flush with excitement. 'You can't ride. It's not safe. Reilly didn't know that.' She glared at him as he sauntered over, infuriatingly confident.

'No, Reilly didn't know that,' he said calmly. 'But I'm not talking about galloping through the gorges. A few turns of the round-yard, something light and safe.'

Damn him. Lea pulled him aside from a disappointed Molly and whispered furiously, 'With Molly there is no such thing as safe. Kids can fall off their own feet. Her blood is so thin it may not clot if she's injured.'

Reilly turned to look at his daughter's enormous, disenchanted eyes. Lea's gaze followed. There was something painfully sad about the silent way Molly accepted disappointment. So horribly stoic and familiar; her heart compressed like bellows.

Oh, God…

'What if she rode with me?' Reilly turned back to Lea, correctly interpreting Molly's bleak expression. Part of her bristled that he was circumventing her authority, but she saw nothing but compassion in his eyes. Then he spoke more quietly. 'I don't want to let her down.'

Lea blinked. A father that didn't want to disappoint—what a novelty. She imagined her little girl, high on the back of one of the horses she adored, tucked in snugly between her father's arms, braced firmly by his strong denim-clad legs.

She looked at the man standing before her. Reilly was a champion rider, being with him would be as safe as being tethered to the saddle. She looked at Molly again and saw the tiniest flame of hope suddenly flicker to life in her young dark eyes.

She wanted to keep it there. Dreadfully.

Her voice was thin as she spoke; it had to squeeze past her heart, which had taken up residence in her throat. 'You'd better take Pan.'

The bigger horse would be more suited to Reilly's size, even though it was a much longer fall from Pan's back. Molly began bouncing on the spot and Lea found herself fielding two gorgeous Martin smiles.

That was hardly playing fair.

'You ride like your own life is at stake,' she warned Reilly through a tight smile, her narrowed gaze locked coldly on his.

He shook his head and vowed on a murmur, 'I'll ride like my *daughter's* is.'

His dark eyes reached out and held hers, confident. Certain. Seductive. Lea's breath hitched deep in her chest. Trusting a man didn't come naturally, but her reserve was cracking. There was something so *solid* about Reilly. Maybe diamond ore wasn't all bad.

He had Pan saddled up and ready to go in just a few minutes. Molly wheezed simply from the excitement and Lea frowned, wondering if she'd made the right decision. But one look at the joy on her daughter's face as she passed Molly up to a mounted Reilly and those doubts dissolved. Lifetime memories started like this. And Molly's lifetime could be a whole lot shorter than other people's.

Their eyes met for a millisecond over the top of Molly's head. Everything lurched into slow motion as Reilly took over care of their precious daughter. Calm confidence leached from his brown eyes. Her heartbeat settled just a bit.

Reilly settled Molly into position, protected in the curve of his body, and moved off. Lea cursed herself for not having a camera handy. Not that she would have got much of a photograph; Molly simply disappeared into the arch of Reilly's body, her stick-thin legs poking out either side of Pan, the child's helmet ridiculously large on her small head. Reilly tucked her hands under his on the reins to give her the illusion that she was guiding the horse.

Pan danced a bit under the unfamiliar male weight, but it seemed to be nothing for a man used to riding broncos. Reilly murmured a few calming words and Pan settled in moments.

So, strangely, did Lea. There was something reassuring about his confidence in the saddle—even out of it—and she let herself stop worrying about Molly's safety and simply enjoyed her experience vicariously.

Two matched pairs of brown eyes concentrated fiercely— Reilly's, glancing diligently between what was ahead and the little person on the saddle in front of him, and Molly's, almost obscured by the large rim of her safety helmet, concentrating on her hands and flicking nervously around the paddock. Her head wobbled under the weight of the helmet and knocked backwards onto Reilly's chest with every step they took. She struggled to keep it level, then gave up and just rested back against his chest.

Reilly's smile twisted and grew.

Round and round the small yard they walked, Molly holding the reins tightly, Reilly holding her hands even tighter and keeping her locked squarely against him. Except for the wobbling head, she had natural balance. Her eyes were like saucers, and Lea didn't think they could widen any further until Reilly leaned down and spoke to her quietly. She looked up at him with unadulterated hero-worship.

Lea's heart squeezed.

Then he turned Pan for the gate and crossed to it, reaching down with his free hand to deftly swing it open into the larger paddock. Sudden thumping kick-started her frozen heart—he was going to run. Lea lurched towards the post-and-rail fencing, panic overtaking her.

'No!'

Reilly paused Pan at the opened gate and glanced back at her. 'Stay in the yard.' Her voice cracked slightly. 'Please.'

His eyes blazed into hers, even across the yard. He barely raised his voice but she heard him. 'She wants to run, Lea. I won't let her come to any harm. I give you my word.'

Lea's heart thumped. The word of a man who was holding

an unborn child to ransom. What was that worth? But then she saw the way he protected every part of Molly with his body, the way she clung to him. Molly had learned to trust her father—or had not yet learned *not* to. Lea couldn't remember the feeling. Her chest constricted with the shadow of old pain. But she stood back and Reilly squeezed the mare with his knees.

Pan moved up to a casual trot and then, as if realising Molly couldn't rise and fall with the horse's staccato rhythm, Reilly increased it. The more comfortable gait meant that he and Molly could move as one as they cantered gently around the larger paddock. On a close pass, Lea saw that Molly's hands had turned in the reins to hold on tightly to Reilly's fingers. He tucked her further back against him. Concern died in her mouth as she saw that Molly was not only perfectly safe, she was loving every moment of her ride.

They smiled and laughed and cantered together, round and round, until out of nowhere Molly began to cry. Reilly turned immediately and crossed the paddock back towards Lea, slowing to a brief trot and then a fast walk. Confusion marred his features as Lea scooted under the fence and walked up to Pan's side. He lowered his tearful bundle straight into her outstretched arms and Molly buried her tears against her mother's shoulder.

His face was tight. 'What did…?'

Lea shook her head and squeezed his calf gently, recognising genuine concern for Molly in his bemused expression. He thought he'd done something wrong. 'She's overwhelmed, Reilly. Exhilaration, fear.' *Hero worship*. 'It's too much. The tears are a four-year-old's way of saying thank you.'

He dipped his head and let the shade of his akubra cover eyes that flicked briefly to her hand on his leg. His Adam's apple worked overtime beneath his tan throat. 'Do you mind if I let Pan have a stretch? I can feel her itching for it.'

No doubt; she hadn't had a good ride for ages. She let her hand drop from his leg and did her best not to feel self-conscious about having touched him. 'Go ahead. The trail leads off from the eastern corner.'

He spun Pan outward and headed straight to the corner of

the larger paddock, giving the mare her head as soon as they were outside the fences. Lea watched them gallop along the long stretch of the paddock towards the trees. Man and horse moved as one, comfortable and at home despite having only just met minutes before, eating up the track. Freed of its precious burden, Reilly's body relaxed, and he tipped forward in the saddle to shift his weight over Pan's centre of gravity and really let her fly.

The last impression Lea had was of the strength and synergy of two beautiful mammals moving together.

Reilly ran the mare until she started to ease. He could have gone twice as far and still not worked off the tightness in his gut. Too much sensation. Lifting Molly onto the horse was the first time he'd properly touched, held, *smelled* his daughter. It had cut straight to his heart—her fragile, warm body so stiff with anticipation pressing against him, clinging to his fingers; her frailty, as though she weighed nothing, which was practically the truth. Her courage in fearing it but doing it anyway.

He'd felt like her father in that moment.

He might not have been present for her first steps, her first tooth or her first words, but he'd given Molly her first ride and, stupid as that was, it felt fantastic. His heart hadn't stopped pounding.

And then she'd started crying. As soon as Lea had explained why, he was reminded how little he was Molly's father. Lea could read her daughter clearly across a paddock; he had been right on top of her but had had no clue he'd overwhelmed her.

He knew nothing. Lea was right; how on earth was he going to raise a child by himself?

That thought neatly brought his mind round to the hot handprint he swore he could still feel burning through his jeans. The way Lea had squeezed his calf to reassure him that Molly was okay; he forced his lips together. He'd asked her to give up her baby. She should resent the hell out of him, not be hurrying to make him feel better.

And he should resent her for her tunnel-vision obsession about stem cells, rather than fixating on how her hand felt on his leg. Besides, compared to what they'd done to each other in the past, touching his calf should have been way down on the Richter scale.

Should have.

His heart was only now returning to its steady beat. He slowed Pan to a gentle walk and circled a big clearing, turning back for the Yurraji homestead. He'd come all this way on instinct. Riding out was what he usually did when he needed to clear his head or work off some steam. It used to be the number one way to get some distance from his visiting parents, neither of whom rode horses—despite what their one-hundred-percent-country publicity photos showed. He'd take off in the care of one of the local ringers far from their reach and not come back until he'd exorcised whatever teenaged demon was at his heels.

Yet suddenly all he wanted to do was get back to his daughter and his…

He straightened his back. What was Lea Curran to him— his ex-lover? His surrogate? Not his friend, that was for sure. She was the woman using him a second time to save a child she'd effectively stolen from him.

And he was Reilly Martin, the king of the circuit, independent and successful despite his lousy upbringing. He relied on no one. It was how he'd taken a sprawling but picturesque dud of a cattle station and turned it into a successful equine breeding-and-training concern: determination. Focus. Being alone.

He shouldn't be itching to get back to either of them. He slowed Pan's progress. His nerve-endings might want one thing, but his mind knew better. Reilly Martin didn't hurry home to anyone.

He was halfway back when Pan's altered gait and sudden nervous dance caught his attention. He looked round and his breath caught deep in his chest: thirty healthy horses of different colours spread out across a distant clearing like a spilled bag of jellybeans.

Lea's brumbies. He reined the mare to a halt and twisted in his saddle to watch the mob.

They were relaxed and grazing while their leader kept a

watchful eye on the stranger on horseback. Reilly's eye moved across the herd just as keenly, recognising some of the finest wild horseflesh he'd ever seen. Then he looked at the stallion and knew why—he was wild, savage and utterly spectacular. Lucky these horses were under Lea's protection or the best of them would be in trucks heading south to the sale yards.

The rest would be on their way to the dog-food factory. Wild horses were at the bottom of the food chain in the north.

The brumbies had the right idea, living in isolation, limiting contact with outsiders, focussing solely on the business of survival. And the continuation of their mob.

Survival and family. Family and survival. There was something in that.

Reilly calmed Pan and turned her for the homestead. Maybe there was a difference between wanting and needing. He *wanted* to get to know his daughter, and if his explosion of sensation for little Molly during their ride was any indication, one visit a month was not going to be enough. But he'd agreed to it and he'd written it up in the contract that Lea had signed. She had no obligation to offer him more and, despite the brief rapport of this morning, he doubted she'd be in a hurry to have him around.

He looked back over his shoulder at the disappearing brumbies and squinted as an idea began to take shape.

CHAPTER SIX

Was it mid-October already? The scorching temperatures confirmed it—the dying weeks of the dry season; everything bleached and crunchy, wildlife lean, water-sources scarce; the land beneath her feet gasping, with air hot and dry enough to suck the moisture right out of your eyeballs.

A terrible time for a little girl to turn five. But at least Molly had made it that far.

'Happy birthday, chicken.' Lea shook Molly awake an hour earlier than her usual seven a.m. waking-time, but it would give her enough time outdoors with Reilly before they had to retreat indoors from the heat for the first of Molly's three therapeutic naps of the day.

It was Reilly's third monthly access visit; three-and-a-half months since she'd been impregnated with his child. With Molly's stem cells. Lea rubbed her hand down her belly, looking for signs of development. If not for the ongoing nausea and test results, she wouldn't really believe she was pregnant at all.

Five years and many months ago, she'd paid exhaustive attention to every change in her body, every twinge in her belly as the extraordinary miracle of pregnancy had unfolded. This time, she was doing everything she could *not* to look inwards. Not to obsess on the tiny being growing inside her. She was taking care, of course—eating the right things, avoiding the wrong things, resting—to ensure that the stem cells she was making would be as healthy as possible for Molly.

But, other than that, she was doing her honest best to forget that there was a life growing in there at all. It was going to get harder once it started to move around, started to engage with her body, to mess with her mind. But for now, while it really was just growing cells, she could almost forget it was there at all.

If she concentrated.

'Is Reilly coming today?' Lea helped a bouncing Molly peel off her nightdress.

She sighed inwardly at the excitement in her daughter's eyes. Reilly's September visit had been heaven for Molly, but a nightmare for her mother. It seemed the energy he was putting into Molly had to come from somewhere, and that meant from Lea. He'd barely engaged with her all day last month and, when he had, it had been critically civil. And entirely cold.

But Molly's bad case of hero worship hadn't diminished any with the passing of another month. If her five-year-old's infatuation had lasted this long then it was no passing fad.

Lea should know. She'd caught herself thinking about Reilly once too often these past weeks. Of the crescent-moon wrinkle that appeared in his left cheek when he smiled. Of his long, artistic fingers. On the up side, it was a tremendous distraction from not obsessing about the life growing inside her, but she really didn't want him in her head at all.

In less than six months, she'd be handing over his baby and resigning herself to seeing it only occasionally, which was almost worse than not seeing it at all—something she'd seriously considered. She swallowed hard. She had no idea what a Kimberley station-owner was going to do with a newborn infant. Maybe he'd find himself a wife. A nanny, perhaps? Another woman raising her child... Lea's lips pressed together as she tugged Molly's T-shirt down over her bony body.

Not her concern, despite being genetic half-owner of the cell-clump inside her. If she started worrying about that sort of thing, she'd start getting attached. And if she started getting attached...

She ran her fingers through Molly's dark hair to calm it, and confessed on a sigh, 'Reilly's already here.'

The birthday girl exploded out of the room with far more

energy than a child in her condition should and ran out of the timber house.

Lea hurried close behind. 'Molly, walk!'

'Hey!' Reilly caught the human bullet and swung her round and up into his arms, as Molly squealed with delight. It was such a perfect TV moment, and it immediately generated a dense stone in Lea's gut. Molly chattered between wheezes like the willie wagtails that ducked and darted around the horses' feet, high-pitched and in machine-gun bursts. Reilly smiled and nodded in all the right places but Lea could tell by the harried little twist between his brows he had only half a clue what Molly was on about.

She intervened. 'Molly, how about we let Reilly catch his breath a minute? He's only just arrived.'

Molly agreed with a five-year-old's lack of grace and scampered off to visit the chickens in the pen at the side of the house. She greeted them as though it had been a month since she'd seen them too.

Lea's lips twisted. That would put a dampener on any ideas that he was special.

'Is she always like this in the mornings?' Reilly turned to her.

'Only on birthdays and Christmas.'

Reilly's brown eyes met hers. 'You didn't tell me it was her birthday.'

She tossed her thick hair back. 'You didn't ask. Besides, I didn't want you thinking we were angling for a gift. You've only known her five minutes.'

'Fortunately,' Reilly said, leaning into the back of his four-wheel-drive, 'I did the maths. I've been carrying this around with me since last month.'

Lea dragged her eyes off those perfect fitting jeans as he turned back to her, large, pink-wrapped parcel in hand.

'You brought a gift.'

'I did.' He looked more closely at her. 'Is that a problem?'

'I… Gifts between Molly and I are usually smaller.' She regarded the enormous pink present with a sad smile. 'She's never had one quite like that.' *Intentionally.*

He hesitated, glancing towards the chicken yard. 'What did you get her at Christmas?'

'I got her me. I was hers to do whatever she wanted with, all day.'

Reilly tipped his head in that way of his and chuckled. 'That must have been some day for you.'

'Oh, it was. We ate ice cream and redecorated the house with her toys. And we swam at Joyce's pool to cool off, not once but twice.'

His chuckle turned serious as he glanced at the box in his hands. 'Do you want me to put it back in the car?'

Lea blew her breath out slowly. She never wanted Molly to know how much her treatment cost, how deeply it ate into the meagre family budget. She managed everything—just—from the income derived from the investments her mother's legacy had bought. But the ICSI treatment and all the medical costs of a new pregnancy weren't coming cheap, either. She'd already sold off half of her portfolio to pay for her daughter's early treatment. It would be a long time before Molly saw a gift this big again.

She eyed it sadly. 'No. Give it to her. She'll be beside herself.'

Reilly's gaze narrowed as he knocked the four-wheel drive's door shut with his hip. 'Do you need money, Lea?'

Heat flooded up her throat, blazing into her face. Did the man have no sense of the appropriate? She crossed her arms as though it was chilly and not thirty-four Celsius. 'Reilly, you can't ask that.'

'Why not? You're the mother of my child. My *children.* I have a vested interest in…' He stumbled. 'In Molly's well-being.'

'I still deserve the basics of courtesy, and that means not re-minding me of how stinking rich you are.'

He followed her to the house, carrying the ridiculous pink box. 'I'm no better off than half the property-owners in the district.'

'You're better off than *this* property owner.' She took the box from him and set it on the table on the ancient timber porch, conscious for the first time of just how rickety the porch was. She thought of Minamurra's perfectly maintained wrought-iron balustrades, and the freshly polished veranda-timbers, and kicked the dirt off her boots on the ancient boot-pull.

'I'm not judging you, Lea. You've had to raise a child alone. On no income.'

She stiffened. 'Do you want to see a profit and loss statement?' Her hand slipped to her belly. 'To ensure your investment is sound?'

'Lea…' His deep frown should have made him less attractive. 'I don't expect you to foot the entire expense of this. You're carrying my child.'

'Thanks for the reminder.'

'You're *raising* my other child.'

'Molly is *my* child.'

He ignored that. 'I want to contribute financially.'

'I don't want your money. I just want the—'

'The stem cells. Yes, I know. But the contract you signed provided for assistance. What have you done with the money that was transferred to your account?'

She hadn't touched it, knowing that she would be giving it all back at the end of this if—*when*—she could figure out a way to break the agreement. 'I didn't ask you for money.'

'No. You've worked hard to keep my contribution purely biological.'

She struggled for something witty to say. Something sharp. But she couldn't; he was way too perceptive.

'Lea, relax. If you'd give me half a chance, I was working my way round to proposing a business arrangement. A lucrative one.'

Lea moved through into the kitchen and swung the half-filled kettle onto the hob of her grandfather's ancient stove. She turned and leaned back against the kitchen bench. The heat coming off the man in front of her matched the heat of the antique at her back.

'What sort of arrangement?'

'I was hoping to have a look at some of your stock.'

She frowned. 'The brumbies? Why?'

'I'm looking for some new breeding lines. I'm aware that you have a different line from most of the others in the district.'

Yeah, wild horses that others would shoot in a heartbeat. 'The horses aren't mine to sell. They're wild; they just live under my protection.'

'You're one of the only properties around here with fences.'

'They're not to keep the horses in. They're to keep opportunists out.' Most poachers wouldn't exactly knock at the front door.

'Then your horses aren't wild.'

Lea frowned. 'Not for lack of trying. In all other ways, I encourage them to be wild. It's make or break on Yurraji.' As devastating as it was to come across one that *hadn't* made it. Anything less and they'd lose all of their wild behaviour. The behaviour that made them Australian brumbies.

Reilly perched on her timber kitchen-island, looking unconcerned. 'I'm interested in sourcing one stallion and two mares. I'm willing to pay you above market-rate for them,' he offered.

Lea frowned. Money again—was that all he was about? 'I told you, they're not mine to sell.'

Exasperation leaked through his words. 'Then I'll make a donation to their upkeep. Or pay for some kind of improvement. I assume you do occasionally like to make improvements?'

Her throat tightened against the criticism of her family home. 'This house was good enough for my grandparents and my mother. It's good enough for my child.'

My child.

He didn't bite. Just stared steadily at her. The more he waited, the more curious she became about his proposal, offensive as it was. The idea of a donation was nibbling at her resistance. Her inner accountant started paying attention—funds that might go to Molly. 'Are you talking about sale or loan?' she hedged.

'Loan. Only until their offspring wean. I'd work from second-generation stock and then you could have the founders back. Release them back to the mob to live out their lives.'

Lea paused, not because she wanted his money, but because it was rare to find someone who thought brumbies had value outside of a tin can. The thought that a little of the wild bloodline might end up in every station in the district was perversely tempting.

The deep voice grabbed at her hesitation. 'Tell you what, why don't we discuss this on the trail? I'd like to look at your stock.'

'They're *not* my stock, and they don't exactly hang out near the homestead. You'll have to ride out quite a way.'

Bark-coloured eyes assessed her. 'Minamurra's ten times Yurraji's size. By my standards, they're practically corralled.'

And just like that, Lea's willingness to play nice evaporated. Her land may be small compared to his, but it was particularly stunning; her grandfather had chosen it for its mix of natural bush, red-rock ravines, rocky pools and spectacular terrain. Its terrain was too undulating and its boundaries too small to be of interest to the mega-graziers in the region, but it was perfect for wild horses—deep, thick cover and plenty of water sources even in the dry season. It was paradise on earth for her. And would be for her children.

She slapped herself mentally. *Child.* Singular.

Her skin tightened. *Corralled.* Still, she'd tolerate Reilly's condescension if he wanted to help develop a local bloodline from wild-brumby stock. Blood seemed that much more important to her these days.

She took a deep breath. 'When would you like to go out?'

They had to tear Molly away from her gift to take a nap, but she fell asleep within minutes. Reilly's heart had clenched at the saucer size of her eyes on realising the parcel was for her. His own childhood had been full of expensive, exciting gifts that cluttered up his enormous bedroom. That had been delivered by courier. What he wouldn't have given for a Christmas gift like Molly's last one: a single day of his mother's undivided attention.

Yet his very first instinct had been to buy Molly something, the bigger the better. Actually, the best. He'd even driven all the way to Broome to find it.

Was Lea right? Was he trying to build himself up in his daughter's eyes? Would she really remember the expensive *Middleton Stables* miniature horse-and-stall set longer than their special but completely free ride together that first day?

His eyes strayed to Lea, leaning forward and tidying up the mess Molly had made in the living area. The move straightened her back and stretched her long neck and shoulders. Reilly's pulse quickened at the uninvited memory of dragging his mouth up that length of golden flesh, how she'd tasted. His eyes retraced the trail, reliving a hint of the former sensation. Lea glanced up in time to catch his expression. Her gaze tangled in his, wide and alarmed. Unwelcome awareness echoed between them. It settled hot and heavy at the base of his spine. Waiting.

She flushed, and it dawned on him for the first time that he made her nervous.

Interesting.

She stumbled to fill the awkward moment. 'Do you still ride horses? Rodeo, I mean. The broncos?'

'Rodeo, but not the broncs. I ride pick-up now.'

She sat back on her haunches. 'What's that?'

'If anyone gets in any trouble, the pick-up guys ride in and help out.'

'Does that include the livestock or just the riders?'

He tipped his head. That wasn't the first sarcastic comment she'd made about rodeo. It was like she was trying to rev him up. He cleared his throat somewhat uncomfortably. 'You don't approve?'

'Nope. Not a fan of rodeo. Two degrees from animal cruelty, in my book.'

His coffee mug practically frosted over in his hand. 'Is that so?'

She took a deep breath, held his stare. Stood straighter. 'In my book.'

It was strangely stimulating, that mix of fear and courage painted so honestly on her face. His voice dropped a few tones. 'We must read different books.'

His comment triggered an unexpected laugh in Lea. 'Reilly, I suspect we're in completely different libraries.'

He blinked. She didn't do enough of that—laughing. It tumbled from her lips like a waterfall and it birthed a vibrant sparkle in her hazel eyes. The sound warmed him, which made it unacceptable.

'I'm not going to argue with you about the relative merits of rodeo, Lea. I think it's unlikely we'll ever agree on that point.'

'I'm not looking for agreement. I just want to understand how you reconcile your passion for horses with rodeo riding—morally.'

His head snapped around to pin her with his eyes and he spoke softly. 'Much the same way I imagine you reconcile having kept a child from its father...morally.'

He might as well have slapped her. She glanced away and flicked her stricken eyes over to Molly's room to make sure she was still asleep, all brightness draining from her expression. He cursed under his breath. God, he wanted to just ask her, just once.

How did you do it, Lea? How did you convince yourself cheating someone out of a child was an okay thing to do?

That decision didn't fit with the woman he'd seen these past weeks. A quiet, determined woman, entirely dedicated to her daughter. Capable of great sensitivity, nonetheless capable of such deceit. The sudden paleness in her skin silenced him. They weren't yet at a place where he could ask. He'd have to wonder a little longer.

He frowned at that rogue thought.

It implied there'd be more between them than what they had now. But getting to know each other was not part of the contract. They were civil for Molly's sake, and that was where it ended. Lea Curran had had no interest in knowing him over five years ago and if it weren't for Molly's condition she'd have no interest in knowing him now. She'd made her choice. She had her family.

The sperm donor was completely dispensable.

And that feeling was just a little too familiar.

Lea had set herself up for the crack about her morals—she'd practically attacked his first—but she needed to know that he was never going to treat her brumbies the way she'd heard they were treated in the rodeo arena.

The way a person treated an animal said a lot about how they would treat a child. 'She'll sleep for two hours now.' Lea spoke guardedly. 'It's been a big morning.'

'Do you leave her like this often?'

She glanced up, armed for a second accusation, but only saw concern. She reined in her desire to snap. 'It's just the two of us here and I have a property to run. I had to learn early to work fast and efficiently so I can get back to her.'

'If she wakes?'

'She won't, but if she does she knows not to leave the house. She'll play with her toys until we get back. But the heat will force us back long before she starts to stir.'

Reilly mulled that over. 'I guess it's not so different to the latch-key kids in the city. It's just not ideal.'

'There's a lot about people's lives that isn't ideal. We all get by as best we can.'

His bottomless eyes hazed over. 'True enough.'

That look got her attention. 'I can't see you as someone who had to get by much, growing up. The only child of rich and famous parents, heir to a country-and-western fortune.'

His snort was a good impression of Goff's. 'Everything you've just said is what I had to get by.'

Lea dropped her eyes. Who was she to make assumptions about his upbringing? Someone looking at hers from the outside might have thought it had been idyllic too.

They crossed the house-paddock down towards her small stables. Ten in the morning wasn't the smartest time to be going out onto her land but life didn't just stop because it got hot. Really, really hot. The brumbies were out there in the shimmering heat and they were going to have company. Pan and Goff whickered in horsey disbelief when Lea emerged with a saddle slung over her arm. She had a quad bike but, quite apart from finding the idea of sharing the single small vehicle with Reilly unthinkable, it felt like sacrilege to ride it out into the bush. Noisy, twenty-first century, overkill. The quiet communion of her horse would do fine.

Of course on a property the size of Reilly's that was probably an unmanageable luxury. Lea wondered if he surveyed his vast lands by low-flying helicopter. She was very conscious that he'd been driving on his own land for at least a third of the three-hour drive here this morning.

She snuck a sideways glance at him. If she'd been thinking straight all those years ago, she never would have chosen Reilly to walk out of the bar with. In the sparsely populated Kimberley, the Martins were virtually neighbours, even though they lived three and a half hours away. Celebrity near-neighbours too. Everyone knew of them, while they knew almost nobody. But he was Reilly Martin. Exactly the sort of man someone in self-destruct mode would be drawn to.

Passionate. Hard. Casual.

She'd been a gonner the moment she walked into the pub and had seen him and his mates propping up the bar, his champion's trophy amongst the discarded empties littering the bar top. She'd desperately needed to connect with someone in her grief, and he had been all too ready to connect with what he'd assumed was a willing out-of-towner.

While half the district knew Leanne Curran by reputation, less than a handful had actually met her. Only her grandfather knew her as Lea.

Grandad and now Reilly.

She'd relied on that anonymity and had doubled her efforts to lay low after she'd discovered she was pregnant. Molly was the gift she'd never realised she longed for. The healing she'd never thought she deserved. It had taken her a year to get over the anxious fear that Reilly would somehow learn of the unexpected pregnancy, piece together all her ramblings the night they had made love and track her to her doorstep, demanding answers. Demanding his daughter. Funny how things worked out.

Different circumstances, but eerily similar results.

Fifteen minutes later they had saddled up and were walking clear of the yards. Reilly was just about to swing up onto Pan when he paused and looked at Lea. 'Do you… Are you all right to mount?'

Lea stared. 'I've been riding my whole life.'

'Is it safe?'

Oh. Dawn was slow in coming. He was worried for his investment. His child. A thousand snappish replies crossed her mind, but she refused to be played. She hoisted herself effortlessly onto Goff's back, met Reilly's cool eyes and matched them.

'It's safe. Let's go.'

'Not that one,' Lea said, pointing to the alpha male. Then she picked out the alpha female from the grazing herd, the one he'd just had his eye on. 'Or that one. Their loss would cripple the mob.'

'Understood,' Reilly said. 'Shame, though. They're both spectacular.'

They stood flank to flank, both appreciating the beauty of the scene before them. The brumbies picked at the dry grasses while their alpha stood guard.

Reilly moved Pan up and down, scanning the distant cluster of horses. Then he turned to Lea. 'Can you get them running? I want to see their conformation.'

She didn't hesitate; she squeezed Goff with her knees and set off towards the mob. Just loping in their direction was sufficient; the alphas turned and struck off across the clearing, drawing the rest of the mob behind them. It was hardly a stampede, more precautionary than panicked, so Lea was able to swing around the bottom of the group and turn them back the other way. They obliged and made a course straight across Reilly's line of sight.

He should have been watching the horses, but he suddenly found himself thinking of ancient centaurs. Lea moved so fluidly with her mount it was as if they were joined at the pelvis. In return, her horse barely knew she was on his back; he was just happy running wild with the mob. Joy radiated off both of them.

There was something about a woman on horseback.

He tensed. Just not *this* one. The woman who'd kept his child from him.

He dragged his eyes back to the mob as Lea turned them across the clearing for a final pass.

Creating a new bloodline had started as a way to spend more time on Yurraji, to see Molly more intensively. Get to know her properly. But the professional in him couldn't do a half-baked job of it. Like everything he did, he did it to completion. It wasn't hard to see the Arab origins in this lot. It meant they'd have the terrific endurance known in that breed. A quality that would cross well with his stock horses' hardy courage. He picked out the three individuals that would suit best; the secondary stallion and two of the trimmest-moving mares. Careful breeding would bring out the best of all three in their descendants.

Lea cantered back towards him, colour high in her cheeks, a wide smile on her face.

That flushed bliss transported her from ordinary to something else. Her wild brown hair blew out behind her and those enormous eyes, green one minute, brown the next, stood out even in the shade of her akubra. She wasn't going to grace a back-bar calendar any time soon, but as she cantered towards him, relaxed and glowing, he could definitely appreciate what he'd seen in her nearly six years ago. It was speaking to him just as loudly now.

He straightened uncomfortably as she drew close. He had no business appreciating anything about Lea Curran. Definitely not the way her smile transformed her face into something disturbingly beautiful.

'I've made my choice.' The snap was unintentional but he saw its instant impact on her. Her radiant grin bled away and she sat up stiffer in the saddle. Whatever joy she'd had running with the wild creatures, he'd just killed it.

Of course; his particular gift.

'We should get back before it gets any warmer,' she said coolly.

Reilly relaxed into Pan's confident stride and let the mare pick her way behind Goff through the scrub. If Lea's spine straightened any further, it would snap. She certainly harboured no desire for him to think well of her.

In fact, if her body language was any indication, all she was interested in was getting him the heck off her property.

Right now, that suited him just fine.

CHAPTER SEVEN

REILLY returned two weeks after Molly's birthday with a crew of three young ringers, striding down the drive with their saddles and tack balanced on their hips, their hats pulled low against the rising Australian sun. The sort of image that was best replayed in slow motion, Lea decided.

Over and over.

Molly had been just as excited, but for vastly different reasons. And her daughter's rapid pulse wasn't fuelled by pregnancy hormones.

That was all it was. She wouldn't be human if she didn't have some appreciation for a handsome, fit man showcasing his skills on horseback. She didn't have to like Reilly to acknowledge the sheer aesthetics of him.

Lea had watched the men closely, once in the bush astride their own rugged stock-horses, as they made short work of locating the mob and separating out the three animals Reilly had selected. The mounted men were poetry on sixteen legs; they seemed to know each other's moves instinctively and they worked together like, well, like a well-coordinated herd.

Reilly was unquestionably the alpha stallion. The three other men responded to his subtle signals and looked to him for direction. Under his guidance, the whole muster took less than two hours, three horses roped while the rest of the mob had followed their leader far to safety at a gallop.

'You want to name the mares after your sisters?' Reilly

looked at her curiously in the mid-morning light. The captured brumbies were settling in Lea's spare paddock for a week or two while he gentled them ready for the journey to Minamurra.

A few days more, with Reilly being a surly misery in her little piece of tranquillity. Here. With her and Molly. *Just fabulous.*

'Look at them. The small one's slight and joyful, with that beautiful mane and tail, and those big eyes. Sapphire to a tee.' She moved across to get a better look at the Dunn. 'And Golden Girl's caramel coloured, all legs and popular with the herd. That's got to be Anna.'

'Do I detect a note of bitterness?'

'Not at all. I love my sisters. This is my way of honouring them.'

Reilly squinted at her. 'Funny way of showing it.'

'Don't try to work us out. Better men than you have failed.'

He dropped his eyes away just as she saw a flash of interest—his instinctive response to a challenge, maybe? He was certainly fighting it hard enough, judging by the way his fingers worried the leather lead-rope he carried.

But then he said, '*That* I have no trouble believing.' He kept his eyeline suspiciously shy of hers. 'So who do you have in your family that's grumpy and hard to manage? We need a name for the male.'

If he could have called the male Leanne, she knew he would have. She gave him her sweetest smile. 'How about God's Gift?'

Her barely disguised reference to him was only satisfying for two seconds, about as long as it took Reilly to realise she was talking about him. And to smile. Just a hint.

Great. Now he'd think she really thought he *was.* She glanced away.

He slapped his hat on his jeans and chuckled. 'You've held their breakfast, yeah? I want them hungry for this morning's training. Today's all about trust. No thinking. No working. Just trusting.'

Over the next forty minutes that was exactly what it was. Reilly moved around the outside of the yard, approaching the horses with snacks, the fastest way to a horse's heart. He rejected the buckets of carrots and oats at first, saying the brumbies wouldn't even recognise them as food, and he worked with clumps of sweet grasses Lea had cut from the boundary. He quite literally had the wild mares eating out of his hand in under an hour, albeit with wide, rolling eyes, slight trembles and a good deal of shying away. But they always came back. Even Lea had to admit that was something.

Pity he wasn't as good with people as he was with horses. Her eyes kept coming back to him like a magnet to true north.

'Are you going to watch me all day, or have you got something else to do?'

Fierce heat scrabbled up her neck, defensiveness in hot pursuit. But, before she could respond, he went on, 'I realise you don't trust me to have the brumbies' best interests at heart, but it's really not going to be productive if you supervise every moment, waiting for me to stuff up.'

Oh. That was what he meant.

More heat.

Had she been this hot in the last pregnancy? Damn him for causing that defensiveness. She sat up straighter on the old log that was her seat. 'I've never seen a horse being broken in. I'm interested.'

He seemed to consider that. Was he trying to work out if she was on the level? 'I prefer to think of it as *gentling* them, rather than breaking them in.' His hand worried his akubra. 'I like my horses workable but spiritually whole.'

Spiritually whole. Not a sentiment she'd expected to hear today from him. He'd practically summarised her entire life philosophy in that one sentence. Her pulse kicked up.

The complexities of Reilly Martin weren't getting any less as she got to know him.

She grew hypnotised by the slow, low tone of his voice as he went back to work, crooning the skittish horses into a relaxed state. She was entranced by the confident stroke of his long fingers along the horses' trembling hides. More than once, she caught herself rubbing low on her belly in time with his measured, reassuring words, and even the now-daily nausea seemed to settle a bit in response. Maybe their child knew its father's voice?

Her breath caught. *His* child.

Lea pulled her trembling hand away and tucked it into her pocket as she lurched to her feet, suddenly loath to stay a moment longer in his influence. The dainty Sapphire shied away violently from the sudden movement just as Reilly was reaching up to stroke between her ears.

He glanced his irritation at her. 'How about some drinks, Lea?'

How about getting the heck away from these horses, Lea?

Her land. Her horses. Her training yard. But he was giving orders. Lea cursed him under her breath as she turned tail and stomped back to the house, cheeks flaming. She checked in on a napping Molly and then headed for the kitchen fridge. Bush code; a good host wouldn't let a guest expire from dehydration on their property.

When she crossed the house-paddock back towards the training yards, a jug of icy juice weighing heavily in her hand, Reilly was nowhere to be seen. She hissed. The man was infuriating even when he wasn't present. Did he want a drink or not?

She crossed around Goff's stable and stumbled to a halt.

Reilly crouched by the horse trough in the yard next to the brumbies using his battered akubra to pour hatfuls of cold water over his searing head while Goff looked on, appalled to find a human in his water trough. The water ran down Reilly's face and glued his T-shirt to his broad shoulders and chest like a wetsuit.

Lea scrabbled back out of view behind the stable wall, her heart pounding in seismic pulses. Again, it was just aesthetics. Reilly was a very handsome, very well built man, for all his many faults, and she'd explored that body up close once.

Blame it on muscle memory.

She just had to separate Reilly the memory from Reilly the actual man. Two very different people. The curious twisting deep down low would be funny if she wasn't so very appalled. Damned hormones. You'd think she'd never met a good-looking man before.

Lea forced a smile to her face and walked out from behind the stable. If he saw her flushed cheeks, hopefully he'd discount it as the heat talking. It was certainly a legitimate excuse. Sweat trickled down between her breasts even now.

'Drink?'

'Thank you.' He took an empty glass from her and she filled it, maintaining a smile that would have done the Stepford wives proud. She leaned on the post-and-rail fence of the paddock, trying to look casual while he drank.

The drone of cicadas almost morphed into a mocking chorus in the awkward silence.

Conversation; normal people would be making conversation here. Not a single inspired thought popped into her head. Lea Curran—debating champion of Pymrose Ladies' College and the girl voted most likely to defend herself in court—was left absolutely speechless.

Worse than speechless—*thoughtless*. Unless it was to think about how those lips currently wrapped around her best glassware had felt against hers. Shivers of memory converged, making her lips tingle. She licked them, half-expecting to taste him there. The thought caused a pang deep in Lea's belly.

She gasped and shot her hand to her stomach.

Reilly stepped up to her in a flash, dropping her best glass. God's Gift took off across the paddock, bucking his protest just once and setting the mares off.

'Are you okay?' His hands immediately went round her.

'I'm fine… It's nothing.' Lea hoped it was nothing. Was that biting sensation a problem, or just her over-charged body's response to Reilly? Too early for a kick, surely? The baby's legs would barely be formed.

Not a baby, just cells. A treatment for Molly.

'You should step back.' He wrapped one large hand around her upper arm and drew her away from her own fence. It was gentle, yet not gentle.

She shrugged free of him. 'I'm pregnant, Reilly. Not impaired.' She bent to retrieve the glass and, when she stood, she glared at him, frustrated. 'Do you wrap your mares up in cotton wool when they're pregnant?'

His silence was telling.

'Didn't think so.'

She stomped off and felt Reilly's eyes on her the whole way.

Travelling three hours daily for two weeks to train the brumbies must have been brutal on Reilly. He must have been leaving his own property at three in the morning in order to be trundling down her drive at sun-up. But Molly loved it and Lea could see no signs in Reilly of anything other than professional focus. He was in his element.

They worked together for five hours solid each morning until the Kimberley sun forced Lea into the relative cool of the house and Reilly back into his Land Rover and home to Minamurra for some time in the office, until early evening when it started to cool off again and he could work his own horses.

That was the beauty of the end of the dry season. The midday temperatures chased you indoors to deal with life's admin. To catch up on all the work you'd let slide during the fertile, blue-skied dry season when all you wanted to do was swim in waterholes filled with fresh, cold water down off the plains or ride through wildflowers and lush, green growth that had sprung to life around about June. Trying to avoid the tourists.

It was the time Lea paid bills, studied her investments and planned her budgets for the coming year. That process was very different this year, excising the last of her investment income to go towards the ICSI, the extra medical. Molly's treatment. Everything was planned down to the last detail. She liked to have her ducks more than in a row; she liked them lined up, labelled and with individual-output quotas.

She really didn't do spontaneous.

Which was why she was bemused to find herself crossing the house-paddock halfway through the morning with a toasted bacon sandwich on a plate. An unexpected, unsolicited sandwich. It was enough to force her feet to a halt.

She was feeding Reilly.

Was it some kind of nurturing kick she was on because of the life growing inside her? She took a mortified step back towards the house, then stopped, thoroughly rattled. She moved to the fallen log that doubled as a bench seat looking over her back paddocks and quietly laid the plate down. The worms in her worm-farm would devour it later.

She'd be damned if she was going to start catering for the likes of Reilly Martin. He was already making himself far too comfortable in her life.

He looked up as she approached, empty-handed. Her smile felt as tight as her chest. 'What are you working on?'

He fiddled with a length of soft lead-rope. 'I need to move faster with this training. I want them floatable by Friday. Today Sapphire's going to learn about tethering.'

Lea frowned. Maybe he was as keen to get out of here as she was to have him gone. She stared at the beautiful, trusting mare.

'Would you like to meet her? Officially?'

Her face must have given her answer, because he stepped aside and let her close. Was this some kind of apology for his overreaction yesterday? She gently moved up to the skittish brumbie and took the food Reilly offered.

He stepped in behind her. 'Hold the food out, but don't point it straight at her, let her come to you.'

Sapphire's nostrils immediately started twitching and her ears turned towards Lea's outstretched hand. Her long face followed and finally her front quarters gravitated unerringly towards the food.

Reilly reached around Lea as the horse moved over and his large hand ran gently along her twitching hide. Lea lifted hers alongside it. Together they stroked their hands gently down Sapphire's long, furred coat, Lea crooning to the nervous mare all the while. Reilly shifted position so he could drop his arms around her and twist her into the safety of his body the second it might be necessary. His intent was subtle, but she didn't miss it.

Lea forced herself to remember he was protecting his child, not her. Her hand dropped away. 'I'm surprised how far they've come in just a couple of weeks.'

His voice was warm and close above her ear. 'I've learned never to be surprised by the resilience and courage of these animals.' He rounded a rub up over Sapphire's ears. 'Treat a horse well and it will reward you with loyalty and affection for the rest of its life. They're much better than humans in that way.'

Loyalty, honour, affection—not qualities she would have expected him to value. Judging by his body language, his displeasure was not, for once, directed at her. She glanced at the strong hands softly stroking the mare's face, his mind a hundred years away. Yesterday it had all been about Reilly's hard angles and pretty face; today it was his gentle patience. This appreciation yo-yo was becoming predictable.

But if he wasn't having a crack at *her*, then...? She turned her head up to him. 'Were your parents not like that?'

Dark eyes slid away from Sapphire and onto Lea, but his hands continued to reassure the mare. He stared down at her hard. 'What makes you think I'm not talking about you?'

She fought away the heat that started to rise. 'I'd take it as a given that you are. But you've only known me a few years. That sentiment sounds like it was born in childhood, not recently.'

He stepped away then thrust her the lead-rope.

'Can I take that as a no?' she huffed.

'Honey, you can take that however you want.' He turned away to reach for more carrots.

Lea's mind immediately joined the dots. It was not the first time he'd avoided the subject by bristling. A hint of a memory from over five years ago fed her impression that things hadn't been rosy at the Martin homestead. Something he'd said that she couldn't quite remember... Something about his parents.

She should leave it; let him have his privacy. 'I'm just curious about your childhood. You never really talk about it.'

Dark eyes swung back to her. 'Just because I don't talk about it with you doesn't mean I don't talk about it.'

She felt the sting of his judgement deep in the thick skin she'd developed over the years. It was an all too familiar bite. Watching him with her horses, it was getting harder to picture him as the careless, brainless saddle-jockey she'd believed he was. Somewhere in the past couple of weeks she'd started to care what he thought of her.

Not very much, judging by his tone.

She took a deep breath. 'Reilly, you're now in Molly's life and she's bonding with you. It's not entirely unreasonable that I'd try and get to know a bit more about you. To understand what makes you tick.' *And whether you're a ticking time-bomb.*

He kept working. 'Funny, I can't recall there being a clause requiring deep and meaningful conversation in our contract.'

She bit back the temper. Breathed deeply. 'Reilly…'

'Are you looking for skeletons in the Martin closet, Lea? To protect your daughter from hurt? Well, let me ask you this one…' he spun square on to her '…how is Molly going to cope growing up with the town outcast for a mother?'

Lea gasped. Reilly barrelled on relentlessly. 'Have you considered what it does to a child to have notorious parents? How invisible it can make you feel? How alone? Half your school friends teasing you and the other half wanting something from you? Especially when your parents are famous. And wealthy. Maybe you should be looking more closely at your own issues rather than digging for mine. *You're* the rod Molly's back will have to bear.'

Lea's heart thumped hard enough to hear in her voice. She willed her heartbeat to slow down. Every part of her wanted to jump on his hurtful words, to strike back, as she'd watched her father do. But it had never really worked for them, had it?

She used the time it took to get her pulse back under control to drag her erratic thoughts into some kind of order. 'I do think about that, actually. And then I remember that if I can just keep her alive long enough to get to school age I'll be doing well. It's easy to push everything else back.'

Reilly's eyes softened. He swore at himself and slid a large hand around her upper arm. His strength leached into her. 'We'll get her to school, Lea. And to uni. And to have her own kids in school.'

Lea couldn't help the tears that prickled at that extraordinary thought. She forced a tight, watery smile. She'd never allowed herself to imagine Molly as a mother of her own child. Her throat thickened. 'She'd be a brilliant mother.'

'She's had good training.'

Lea blinked, astonished.

'I may not like how Molly came into being, Lea, but there's no doubting that you've done an amazing job with her. Before her sickness and since.'

Thumpety-thump; there went her heart again. 'You never knew her before.'

'I can see how she must have been. The way she's so confident. Respectful. Amazingly responsive to authority. That's down to you. You've raised her well.'

Lea stared, a single tear spilling over. Reilly swiped it away with his thumb. She frowned at him, confused. 'Thank you, Reilly.'

'Are you so surprised I would think it? I'm not a monster, Lea.'

She realised she'd stopped thinking of him in 'monster' terms weeks ago. A pleasant shiver marched up her spine. 'I should get back to her. Good luck with Sapphire.'

Lea marched, stiff-backed, up to the house and Reilly watched her go, torn. He hadn't expected the flashes of softness he'd seen in her over the past couple of weeks. She was as sharp as a tack—another thing he could feel himself appreciating—but vulnerable with it. It drew him in, like the bad old days. It was the same quality he'd responded to in that bar. He'd recognised the signs of an animal in distress.

He wasn't interested in bonding with her now. He just wanted to get on with the business of moving these horses to Minamurra. Of making a baby. He stroked the skittish mare while its nostrils flared wildly.

Business, like the rest of their relationship.

Not a relationship. He was Molly's father and the biological father of the child growing in Lea's fit, glowing body. He didn't owe her a thing that he hadn't already delivered in spades. Yet he found himself worrying about her out here alone with Molly. The two of them isolated on the wrong side of the ridge, living on a property that Lea could barely manage on her own.

Maybe she needed to find a husband. Get some help. She wouldn't want to—Lea Curran was not a woman who settled unnecessarily—but maybe it was what she needed.

The thought of another man raising Molly frosted his blood. Someone else teaching her to ride and how to do long division. And the thought of another man touching her mother's perfect skin—

His whole body jerked upright. Sapphire tossed her head and trotted off, tail swishing in agitation. *Whoa...* Where had that thought come from? And why was it so slow to drain away?

He didn't need to start indulging thoughts of that kind, and he didn't need to start having in-depth discussions about his family with a woman like Lea Curran. That wasn't going to help anybody.

He pulled his hat down harder on his head, as if to squeeze inappropriate thoughts out, and set about luring the mare again.

Two days later Reilly released God's Gift to canter off to the middle of the paddock. 'I'd like to leave the transporter here overnight, loaded with food and backed up to their yard, so the brumbies can explore it at their own pace. Tomorrow we get them on the truck and over to Minamurra.'

Sensible, except... 'How will you get home tonight?'

The look Reilly gave her was cautious. And loaded. 'I was thinking of staying here.'

'No.' Absolutely not. 'I'll drive you home.'

'It's a six-hour round trip, Lea. You will not.'

'You've been doing it every day.'

'I'm not four and a half months' pregnant. I can doss down in the tack compartment of the transporter.'

Lea had seen that compartment; it was designed for stableboys and equipment, not for six-foot-plus men made of solid granite. 'God's Gift's not going to go in there if he can smell you.'

'We'll give it a try.'

She chewed her lip. Nightfall was still nine hours away and the heat meant they'd finished training for the day. 'What will you do for the rest of the day?' The thought of him hanging around at a loose end for hours was unsettling.

He shrugged. 'What do you and Molly normally do during the heat of the day?'

Lately? While Lea's body adjusted to supporting a new life and the weather was so disgusting? 'Sleep. Read. Swim.'

He stripped his hat off to wipe sweat from his forehead. Even hat hair and heat glow didn't diminish his looks, all angles and equine lashes.

'A swim sounds good,' he said. 'Where do you go?'

There were a handful of swimming pools in the district, of the installed kind, but most landowners had access to natural pools that formed at the base of rocky outcrops. The tourists dominated the safe public ones that still had water in them after a long, hot dry season, and crocodiles dominated the rest.

'Joyce's Pool at the far edge of Yurraji is spring-fed and runs all year round.' In the wet season it more than ran, it flooded with rain-wash, and created a spectacular billabong wetland filled with life. But in the dry season it subsided back to being smaller, deep and cold, fed directly from the aquifer.

And it was very, very private.

Lea's heart sank that she was going to miss her daily swim. And on a sticky scorcher like today too. She sighed. 'I'll give you directions.'

'I don't want to run you off your swim. We can all go.' His glance was casual. 'I'd enjoy seeing Molly swim.'

Right. An afternoon with Reilly Martin at the most secluded and pristine corner of the property—out of the question. Her hormones had been making things quite difficult enough without spending a few hours watching him cavort semi-naked in a natural spring. Even with a pint-sized chaperone.

Reilly raised his voice so Molly could hear him from the porch where she played with her Middleton ponies. 'What do you say, kiddo? A swim at Joyce's Pool?'

'Yeah!' Molly did her happy dance, no doubt delighted at the prospect of showing her new friend her favourite swimming spot. Or floating spot, in Molly's case, given her reliance on industrial-strength floatation aids.

Reilly noticed Lea's reluctance and his lips thinned. 'Come on, Lea. You couldn't be in safer company.'

Hurt broiled in her chest. Because he drew the line at hitting

on a pregnant woman? Or because he had no interest whatsoever in her, pregnant or otherwise? She gave herself a mental
pinch. What did it matter? She shouldn't care whether he
looked at her as a woman or as a brood mare. The man wanted
a swim. So did she. So did Molly.

'Okay. Give me twenty minutes to find a swimsuit.'

To find *a* swimsuit. Not *my* swimsuit.

Lovely Lea Curran usually swam naked. Realisation hit
Reilly out of nowhere and the unwanted, illicit image struck
straight for his groin. Why wouldn't she? Her own land, her
own pool, her own rules, and a five-year-old who wouldn't
know the difference. Only Lea and the wildlife for a hundred-
thousand lonely acres.

Never mind that the occasional lost tourist might stumble
upon a naked nymph drifting in the water. If they were smart
they'd look their fill and then disappear back into the bush with
that mental postcard for ever.

Welcome to the Kimberley!

Lea's hands moved surely on the steering wheel of her beat-
up old four-by-four. Other than the air-conditioning, it was
stripped back to nothing, a typical north-west working vehicle,
and it handled the rocky track like it was on four sturdy legs.
Lea wasn't kidding about the pool being on the far side of her
property. They'd set out diagonally across Yurraji a lifetime ago.
It was slow, rough going, picking across the brutal terrain.
Molly had become increasingly grizzly as the minutes had
ticked by, even with the air-con on full.

Joyce's Pool must be something special to make this journey
worth while all season.

That swim was looking pretty good. With or without swimsuits.

The naked swimmer fit the image of the wild, free spirit he'd
been expecting to find. A leopard didn't change its spots no
matter how hard it was working to cover them up. So Lea
galloped across the flats with her hair flying, and she liked to
swim naked in ancient watering-holes. That fit. That was the
woman that might get the district's back up over animal-rights

issues. That would raise a child defiantly on her own. That would struggle to make friends in the conservative grazing-country. That would become a target. He almost felt sorry for that woman.

If not for the fact that that same woman had also cheated him out of a child.

The pool, when they rumbled out from between thick scrub, was like a blue-green oasis. The Kimberley red rock had eroded to form pastry layers of pure, hardened magma, an ancient staircase down to the glassy emerald sheet that was the undisturbed waterhole surface.

He had nothing like it on Minamurra, despite his station's size. 'It's beautiful. How long have you been coming here?' he asked.

'Grandad first brought me when I was about eight. Just before Dad packed us off to boarding school.' A shadow crossed her face.

What put that there—memories of boarding school, her grandad or her father? And why did he care?

They parked the vehicle and walked the remaining distance down to the water. It felt natural to Reilly to pick up a dozy Molly and save her the walk. Even the surrounding birds were sleeping off the worst of the midday heat, making the constant drone of insects the only sound for miles.

Towards the back of the pool, a granite overhang threw some welcome shade onto the rock shelf and provided protection from the sun blazing in the deep-blue sky. It felt three degrees cooler in the shade, so Reilly dropped their gear and his daughter there.

'Will you watch Molly? I always walk the perimeter, just to be sure,' Lea said, setting off around the waterhole. There was a shelf of rock right the way around, stretching back to the scrub that grew in the sandy earth bounding the rock. Nature's pool-decking. Molly sat completely still on a nearby rock, obviously accustomed to this routine and knowing what her instructions were.

'Have you ever found anything?' Reilly asked when she returned.

'It's purely precautionary. The only things living in that

water are marron and they're much more interested in what
settles on the bottom than what's swimming in the top.'

'But you still check for crocs?'

She looked at him. 'With the early onset of the dry season,
wouldn't you?'

She had a point. Giant saltwater crocodiles surfed the high
waterways further inland every year, but they got stranded here
if the waters receded too early. They crept around between
inland pools getting hotter and hungrier and more desperate
until the rains returned and opened up their aquatic path back
to the coast to feeding grounds.

Finally, she was done. Reilly watched her staring into the
blue-green depths for a moment before recognising her delaying
tactics. She didn't want to be the first one to get her clothes off.
Her reluctance was oddly sweet. He started to pull off his shirt,
then stopped and frowned. He kept himself in good shape, and
revealing his body to a woman was normally a cinch, but
flashing his flesh to Lea seemed different now. Awkward.

Standing here fretting about it was stranger still. What was
going on with him? It was ridiculous to be shy with a woman
who knew every inch of him, biblically speaking.

Reilly tossed his hat onto their belongings and reached his
arm over his head to yank his T-shirt over it defiantly. Lea
turned away but slowly did the same, unbuttoning her ever-
present denim shirt and peeling it back to reveal the swimsuit
she wore underneath. He tried not to stare.

It was stupid to be disappointed with a one-piece, especially
one that she filled out so admirably, but some deep, honest part
of him had been holding out for a bikini so that her stomach
was bared. He'd not noticed it under her usual farm-wear, but
the changing shape of her belly was clearly visible in a swimsuit
under the teal fabric. He ripped his fascinated eyes away, his
heart pumping.

His child was in there. Safe. Warm. Loved.

That last thought had him frowning.

He'd changed into shorts back at the property so all he
needed to do was kick off his shoes and he was good to go.

Some ancient sense of chivalry told him he should get straight in. If there was danger to be faced, he should face it first. Wasn't that what a chivalrous man would do? It wasn't a quality he had a lot of experience with.

The water swallowed him like a living creature. The first five centimetres were comfortable enough but below it was frigid. The kind of cold straight from the guts of the earth. His breath hitched in, and other bits of him hitched up for survival. Not that there was anything to protect any more.

He shook the miserable thought off and stepped away from the rock shelf to the deeper water. As he did, he heard a hiss as Lea stepped into the water. The curse that followed was not particularly ladylike; he smiled.

Reilly let himself drift into the centre of the pool. It wasn't enormous, but was so green and deep it could be harbouring Nessie herself. He thought his days of adrenaline rushes had died with his Suicide Ride career, but he had a little one now at the thought that he really had no idea what might be in the water with them. But Lea's confidence was contagious. She knew what she was doing.

Molly stood patiently in the shade beside the water, all floated-up, waiting for her mum to swim over to her. The rock in Reilly's gut threatened to pull him under. Without clothes, the poor kid was a pure stick with wasting, pale flesh. If Lea's plan didn't work...

She reached up from the pool and lifted Molly gently into the arctic water.

Childish squeals ricocheted through the rock gully and pierced at least one of Reilly's eardrums. But then they subsided as Molly's body warmed up until she too floated quietly, the sun heating her upper half as the water cooled her lower half. For long minutes he and Lea drifted around the pool in opposition, keeping a wide berth from each other. But slowly, subtly, Reilly let himself float closer. Made himself float closer.

For the first time ever, the silence was bothering him. He glanced at Molly and saw that her eyes had drifted shut. Her third nap already today, probably due to the hot, uncomfortable car ride.

He frowned. 'Can I ask you something—in the spirit of getting to know each other?'

Lea's smile was tight but resigned. She could hardly protest, given it was her line from earlier.

'What made you want to raise a child alone, outside of a relationship?'

It was a risk, a huge risk; this could go two ways. He held his breath and hoped she'd answer. He wanted to put this question to rest. 'You were young. Outnumbered twenty-to-one out here in the bush. You couldn't find a husband?'

She swam on for a moment and he thought she might not answer, and then she rolled onto her back. The half-circle of rock surrounding the pond acted like natural amplification, meaning she didn't even need to raise her voice to be heard. The sound-waves raced across the surface of the water to his ears. He drifted closer to Molly just in case she got in any trouble as she slept.

Lea watched him carefully across the glittering surface and glanced at her daughter. 'I'm not looking for a husband.'

Present-tense noted. 'You don't like men?' He knew that wasn't true, she'd liked him a lot several years ago. Many times over. But it didn't hurt to check.

Lea laughed, tight and low. 'My formative impressions of husbands and fathers weren't very positive.'

He nodded. 'Your father. You told me in the motel he'd died recently.'

She watched him carefully across the glittering water. 'Actually, his funeral was that morning.'

Reilly frowned. 'What were you doing in a bar?'

Her smile was tight. 'Celebrating.'

Right! If not for the pained shadow in her eyes he would have believed her. He remembered the agonised tears he'd interrupted in the motel bathroom when she'd thought she was alone. 'He's the reason you're single?'

'His example didn't really fill me with confidence in the male of the species.'

Hmm. There was a discussion for another day… 'Hence your decision to go it alone.'

'I've never regretted having Molly.'

There was something in her tone. 'But you do have some regrets?'

She dropped her eyes briefly. Colour spiked up her jawline. 'I regret the circumstances of her conception.'

Interesting. She'd already said she wouldn't do it like that again.

'Lying to me?'

'It wasn't a lie.' True; technically it had been an omission. She met his eyes. 'But I wasn't honest, either. I was too caught up in what I needed to think about the ramifications. I'm sorry for that.'

He risked the question. 'Do you regret choosing me?'

Caution blanketed her steady gaze. Her eyes sparkled with reflected sunlight. Every part of him wanted to swim in them. He held his breath.

'I regret deceiving you.'

But not 'choosing you'. She might as well have said it. The strangest glow spread inside him. He recognised it from the feeling in the hospital corridor when he'd just become a father.

He cleared his throat and looked at Molly drifting, dead to the world around the pool. 'You never thought a father figure could be important to her some day? Even though it wasn't important to you?'

Lea frowned, her hazel eyes darkening. 'A father is important. But a bad one does more damage than not having one at all. My children will have a mother who loves them, that's what counts.'

Reilly's gut tightened. Children—plural. Was she thinking of backing out of the contract? He sank under briefly to wet his drying hair and cool his response. When he surfaced, she regarded him closely, lifting her chin.

'It's the twenty-first century. Are you so shocked that a woman might want a child without the complication of a relationship?'

Reilly considered that for a moment. 'Not shocked, just… I don't understand how you could do it—manage it alone. Why you'd want to.'

A pretty stain crept up her jaw. 'Curran women are highly

resilient. We can do all kinds of difficult things when we need to.' Reilly grunted. Lea stared at him through arctic eyes. 'For a man who's slept with half the district, you're pretty quick to judge.'

His eyebrows shot up. 'For a woman who's hoping I'll keep my end of the stem-cell bargain, you're pretty fast with the insults.'

Her controlled breathing caused her glistening cleavage to breach the surface of the water and then disappear again. In. Out. Now you see it, now you don't. He dragged his eyes upwards as she spoke carefully.

'Why would you want to back out? Having held your daughter.'

He met her worried gaze. 'I'm not backing out, Lea. Molly's come to mean—' *everything* '—as much to me as she does to you.'

They fell to silence on that profound admission. Lea gave a dozing Molly a gentle shove to send her drifting closer to the pool's edge. Her voice dropped to a murmur. 'Can I ask you something—in the spirit of getting to know each other?'

He smiled.

'The rumours say you slept with your nanny.'

Reilly's brows dipped together. 'I thought you were too much of a pariah to be in on town gossip.'

'Just because no one talks to me doesn't mean I don't hear anything.' She tipped her head to the left as though accessing memory banks. 'Super-famous showbiz parents, dragged you around with them on the road for the first part of your life, until they noticed you were suffering.'

Reilly snorted. 'Or my grades were…'

'Then they left you on the homestead with School of the Air, a housekeeper and a nanny. You drove away every one until you were eighteen…'

'Seventeen.' He took a breath, fought candour with candour. 'Technically they weren't all nannies, the last two were tutors. Every time one left, Kevin and Adele automatically replaced them. I'm not even sure they knew how old I was towards the end there.' He shook his head. 'Who sends a seventeen-year-old boy a Swedish backpacker and doesn't expect trouble?'

Lea's jaw dropped. 'The rumours are true?'

'A Swedish backpacker, Lea? I was seventeen and learning to fit into my skin.'

'She was an adult. Your tutor!'

He waved off her concern. 'She was barely older than me, and she taught me Swedish. And a few other useful things. I taught her about the Kimberley.'

Both her hands went up. 'Stop. My point was supposed to be that rumours hardly ever represent the truth.'

'Oh. It's the truth you want?' *Careful what you wish for.* 'My mother dragged me halfway around the country to show me off, not to keep the perfect family together. I was her prize creation, the poster-child country kid.' He paddled slowly closer. 'They taught me to line-dance from the moment I could walk, and forced me to learn the guitar while my fingers were still pudgy with baby fat. When she dumped me back home it was because I wasn't doing so well in school with all the travelling, and that reflected on them. God forbid she should have a dumb son. Lucky I was good-looking, huh?' His laugh was bitter. 'The revolving door of nannies wasn't about me, Lea. It was about how isolated those poor women felt, stuck out in the bush with a maladjusted kid, a surly housekeeper and two thousand head of steer for company.'

He stopped drifting, practically on top of her. The water should have bubbled where his body nearly touched the furnace that was hers. Every part of him remembered how every part of her had felt back then. This time he didn't shut it off. He used his voice now as he had then, to hypnotise her, to get closer.

'It took me a few weeks, but even I eventually realised it was the wrong thing to do. So I had Grita's contract paid out and I channelled all that youthful exuberance into learning to ride the broncos.' He was loath to break the spell he'd so successfully cast. He could kiss her right now and she'd let him. His lower lip throbbed at the thought. His eyes butterflied over her face. 'So, there you go… Every rumour has a solid foundation in fact.'

Lea blinked, surprised to find herself so close to him. She back-paddled a little, but it seemed reluctant. 'No, it doesn't.

I'm not… I haven't…' She frowned and stared at him in silence, a shadow flitting across her gaze. 'If rumours are seeded in fact, then that means I really *don't* fit well. I've spent years convincing myself it's other people's fault.'

He'd thought her as hard as the granite surrounding them. But her tough outer shell was taking some direct hits lately, and a soft, vulnerable woman hid inside. He was staring directly at her right now.

The problem was she was going to need that strength when the baby came. Even with the stem cells, Molly's treatment was still no sure thing. His chest was band-tight and he decided to go there, pretty sure it would be a conversation-ender.

He dropped his voice. 'What will you do if the treatment fails?'

Lea's face lost some of its colour. She glanced at Molly, who'd woken and was happily singing to herself as she floated around out of earshot in her rubber ring, then back to him. Her eyes were bleak. 'I think it's time to get going.'

'Lea, wait. I'm serious.' His hand shot out to catch her upper arm, baked warm from the blazing sun. Her heat burned into his cool, wet fingers. He lowered his voice further so that Molly wouldn't hear. 'If the stem cells don't work, what will you do?'

Her nostrils flared wildly. He could practically feel the distance she forced between them with her cold look as she whispered. 'I'll bury my daughter under one of Yurraji's ghost gums.'

His stomach clenched. 'And then what?'

How could eyes so full of pain also be so empty? 'Are you worried I'd just keep walking out into the desert? Like I said, Curran women are resilient. I've buried plenty of people I loved. I'd survive.'

She pushed herself into movement and swam past him to the edge of the pool where Molly floated happily.

So finding him really was Lea's last resort, Molly's only chance. He finally believed her. His chest was so tight it hurt to spread his arms, to stroke over to the shallow part of the waterhole and haul himself out of the water. He ignored the sun's warmth as it kissed his cold, damp skin.

He turned to share his thoughts, and then his stomach

lurched up into his throat as his eyes dragged across the length of the pool. He raced to the edge of the rock shelf and reached down to where Molly floated blissfully. He yanked her out roughly with one hand under her shoulder. Molly immediately began screaming.

Lea spun around in the water, fire in her eyes. 'What the…?'

'Give me your hand, Lea.' He had Molly's non-existent weight slung under one arm and he stretched towards Lea with the other.

Her angry gaze raked over him hotly before meeting his own. 'I can manage myself.'

'Your hands, Lea. Now!'

Lea took one look at his face, stretched her hands up towards him and wrapped both hands around his wet one. He willed his body to have the strength, and then he pulled. Lifting up and out at the same time bit into his back muscles, but in just a few seconds her feet were on the red rock-shelf and he was hauling her back from the edge into his body.

She fought him the whole way. 'Reilly, what the—?'

He forced her behind him and surrendered the wailing, wheezing Molly to her mother, backing up further and ignoring Lea's protests. Finally far enough from the water's edge, he dragged mother and daughter around in front of him, keeping them within the protective arc of his arm and forcing Lea's cool body back against his flaming one. He pointed over her shoulder to the far side of the pool in front of them.

'What?' she fairly yelled, struggling to be free. 'What are you doing?'

'There, Lea!' He pointed a second finger after the first, his arms triangulating an exact location either side of her angry gaze. He wasn't going to say it aloud, not with Molly already terrified.

And then she saw it. Her entire body stilled. A dirty smear from the scrub to the edge of the pool, like something large had crawled across there. But it hadn't been there when she had done her perimeter check, and there was no water on the rock.

Which meant it was crawling *into* the pool and not out of it.

She half-turned in his arms but didn't take her eyes off that spot. 'Reilly…'

He let his arms wrap around them both for a heartbeat and then he was shoving them towards the four-wheel drive. Towards safety. It was all he could think about, getting them out. His pulse thundered painfully. 'Get to the truck. I'll get our stuff. Go straight there; go across the high rocks, stay back from the water's edge.'

Lea complied immediately, which was a miracle in itself. As he saw her getting further from the pool, his body dropped some of its urgent tension and he started to notice other things. Things he was stupid not to have spotted before. Like the fact that the insects had all stopped chirping. The birds had all gone.

He kept his eye on the water as he dragged their belongings to the back of the rock wall and bundled them up into his trembling arms. No sign of the crocodile. But it was there, no question. Big, small; it didn't matter. If it had come this far, it was either really hungry or really hot. Either way it was likely to be grumpy and not inclined to share.

And that was not a croc you wanted to mess with.

He backed towards the truck and then took his time picking his way barefoot through the scrub. It wasn't worth the lost seconds to slip his sandals on. His heart was still racing and his legs shook with the after effects of his body's massive adrenaline-dump. It wasn't the same heady rush he'd got riding the broncos—this was darker, stronger—but it had its usual effect on him. The last traces of it zinged around his body and teased his senses. Suddenly his mind filled with the woman clambering into the four-by-four: slim, but unquestionably pregnant, with the slightly convex belly as her body made preparations for the new life in it. Weighty breasts. Healthy glow.

All things beautiful and natural.

That was why she'd felt so damn good tucked into him just now, it was his body's natural chemicals. The momentary survival-high. And she was wet and female and abundantly fertile.

His subconscious had noticed even if the rest of him was in complete denial.

'Must you? That's really not helping me relax.'

Reilly took his eyes from the pocked trail they were bumping along to glance sideways at Lea. She was pointedly staring at where his hands practically strangled her steering wheel. Almost as hard as the white-knuckled ferocity with which she held the passenger-side door handle.

He eased his grip. 'Sorry.'

They'd tumbled into the vehicle wearing nothing but what they'd been swimming in. As a result, Lea sat trembling in the front seat wearing only her swimsuit and her daughter. Molly lay across her, having cried herself to sleep from the fright, and Lea stroked the dark, damp head that rested on her shoulder. Lea had pulled a dry towel around Molly but not herself. She looked cold and uncomfortable, but something told him not to intervene, that she needed to be close to her daughter right now.

Neither of them had spoken in the half-hour since they'd fled the waterhole. It had taken Reilly that long to muddle through the feelings surging through him in the wake of the adrenaline.

Concern. Anxiety. Desperation. Emotions he'd had little experience with in his past. He'd grown up fast on his own on Minamurra and trained himself not to indulge emotions that weren't contributing to his survival. His achievement. He was all about confidence, composure, ambition, courage. It took him minutes even to recognise the foreign emotions. As soon as he did, his heart started to race, and he knew why. For the first time, he had something to lose.

Molly.

And his unborn child.

And, God help him, the woman carrying it.

His mind raced back to the water's edge; the gut-turning fear that had torn through him. Those were not feelings he cared to indulge again any time soon. The thought of leaving them unprotected on a property as wild as Yurraji...

'I want you both to come back to Minamurra with me.'

The unexpected statement at least had the unexpected benefit of bringing a hint of life back to Lea's numb expression. 'What?'

'You'll be safer there. Molly will be safer there.'

'This could have happened anywhere, Reilly. There could be crocodiles in your waterholes too.'

'This isn't about crocodiles,' he said.

No; it's about me panicking because I don't know what to do with all the damned emotion that's flooding me. 'You're over four months' pregnant, and the wet season is right on top of us. You're alone on a property on the wrong side of the ridge with a sick child and no airstrip.'

If she clenched her jaw any harder she'd crack her molars, but that meant she was hearing him. He stared intently at her. Passion was pouring out of him from somewhere he'd never known. 'If you tell me that the roads leading to Yurraji don't wash out in the wet, and that you won't have any trouble getting out of there in a crisis, I'll believe you. I'll never raise it again.'

Reilly knew from driving those pitted roads repeatedly how much water they must see during the wet season. There was only one asphalt road running through all the Kimberley and she wasn't on it. He sensed Lea was incapable of lying—which wasn't the same as always telling the truth. Sometimes she'd just say…nothing.

Like now. She stared at him, trying to outguess him.

'Think about Molly.' Her eyes flared and he knew it was a cheap shot. Lea Curran did nothing *but* think about her child. Her hands tightened on her daughter. 'If something happened to you and you couldn't help her, that's three lives at risk: yours, the baby's and Molly's. Three lives on my conscience.'

'Your conscience? How is this about *you*?'

'I have an airstrip. I have a giant, empty house with a ton of food. Molly will love it at Minamurra.'

'I realise you don't think I do anything, Reilly, but I have a property to run.'

'You run your property wild. It looks after itself.'

'What about Pan and Goff? Who's going to look after them?'

'I'll have them collected. Taken to Minamurra.'

'You will not!'

'You've seen my property, Lea, it'll be like a horse-retreat for them.'

'Because it's big and expensive and covered in reticulated grasses? No, thanks. They're fine where they are. Yurraji may be small, but it's their home.'

Ideas poured out of him. 'Then I'll have someone stay on Yurraji to keep an eye on them and the brumbies. Lea, it's nothing to me to have you stay.'

A dark shadow flared briefly in her eyes and her mouth tightened. 'You've thought of everything.'

'Actually, yeah. It seems the most obvious thing to do.' He felt the track even out and knew they were drawing closer to Lea's home. He slowed the vehicle slightly; he needed a bit more time.

'For five months?'

'Why not? Folk around here do it all the time when they get rained in. Come on, Lea; ride out the wet at Minamurra.' He took a breath. 'With me.'

Clearly those last words didn't hold the same meaning for Lea. She glared at him a little longer. 'And if I wasn't pregnant with your heir?'

Reilly blinked. 'It's not an heir, Lea. It's a child. Our child.'

Hazel eyes flicked away for the briefest of moments. '*Your* child. You asked me to sign to that.'

Reilly stiffened. 'You signed over custody, not your maternal rights. It's your baby too. Another Molly.'

She sucked in a breath so fast she almost hissed. 'It's an umbilical cord to me, Reilly. Nothing more.'

His heart twisted in a knot. *Shades of Adele.* 'You don't mean that.'

'It can't be anything else.' She sat straighter, speaking through a clenched jaw, avoiding his eyes. 'I can't let it.'

'Why not?'

Her nostrils flared, just like God's Gift when he was working up to a thrash around the paddock. 'Do you still want…this?' She indicated her belly below her sleeping daughter.

'What? Of course.'

'Then in less than five months you'll be holding your child in your arms. A tiny living being, snuggled against *your* warmth.'

The image hit him in the solar plexus.

'And I'll be watching it being carried away.' She pinned him with her burning gaze. 'I need to hand that child over to you, Reilly. You can't possibly not have thought about that?' Her eyes dropped, and when they rose again they burned darkness. 'You're many things, but thoughtless is not one of them.'

He frowned. 'I... Isn't it instinctive—to bond? *Can* you turn it on and off?'

She white-knuckled the door handle again, as though the painful outlet was better than what she really wanted to do. Or maybe say?

'Yes, Reilly, it *is* instinctive. I feel that life taking shape inside me. My body's changing to accommodate it, my habits have changed to be half mine and half the baby's. I like chicken, it makes me crave liver. I hate tomatoes, but find myself wanting to chug a vat of salsa. This baby owns me for the next five months. It's part of me.'

'Well, that's good, isn't it?' *Were you always this obtuse, Martin? The woman's trying to say something.*

She nearly burst from not screaming. 'Do you know how hard it is to resist letting myself love this baby? If I let him in, it will kill me to give him up.'

She looked horrified to have verbalised the thought. Her eyes widened, stricken. The sound of hard breathing filled the truck.

Reilly cleared his throat. 'Him?'

She tipped her head up to stare at him through bleak eyes. 'What?'

'You said "him". Is there something I should know?'

Lea's head dropped back down for the longest time. 'No,' she mumbled, her chin resting on Molly's head, her damp, dark hair shielding her face. 'Slip of the tongue.'

Maybe she was more bonded with this baby than she knew. A new kind of excitement rushed through him. 'Do you think it's a boy, Lea? Did your last scan...?'

She sighed. 'I didn't ask at the scan, Reilly. But this pregnancy's so different from Molly's. Maybe?'

For some weird reason, her instincts were the one thing he *did* trust about her. She was such a part of the land, of nature, it seemed reasonable that her heart would know what she was carrying even if her head didn't. His chest began to hammer.

A son. And a daughter. Considering he was a man who'd never had either, a matched pair would be extraordinary. The idea of a little boy-version of Molly running around stole all the air from his body.

His head came up, shamed. He was a lousy human being.

'No, I haven't really thought about how you are going to hand the baby over.' In fact, he hadn't ever visualised her handing the baby over at all. Not because he seriously thought she wouldn't honour their agreement, but because he simply hadn't considered them parting. Stupid. His brows dropped. 'Of course you will. As soon as you have your cells.'

'*Molly's* cells.' Wide, hazel eyes stared at him. 'I signed your contract, Reilly, but it doesn't mean I agree with it. I'm doing this because you're leaving me with no option. I'm doing it for Molly.'

Reilly sagged. While he was being handed the most precious gift possible, she was being asked to tear part of her soul out. Who was he kidding? He hadn't asked Lea to surrender the baby, he'd *required* it.

Who was the bigger monster here—Lea for neglecting to tell him about Molly, or him for putting such a condition on the saving of a child's life?

Self-disgust leached through him. He was going to rip Lea's heart out so that he could have a child. An heir. It was all about what he wanted. How was he any different from his mother? He swallowed the large lump that formed in his throat and acted before he changed his mind.

He reached over and took her icy hand. 'Then do one more thing for Molly—come to Minamurra. Let me look after you all until the baby's born.' He squeezed her fingers. 'Just a few more months.'

Lea looked entirely distracted by the hand on hers. 'I'm pregnant, Reilly. My body is not my own any more and it's making strange decisions. I'm not comfortable being in someone else's house while that happens.'

He stared at her, considering. 'You think I'm not accustomed to pregnancy? I breed horses for a living.'

Lea glared, some of her usual spirit returning. 'What a flattering comparison, but hardly the same thing—unless you have a horse doubled over your loo every morning bringing up its chaff and apples.'

Concern creased his forehead. 'Are you still suffering morning sickness? Shouldn't it have ended by now?'

'Have you been reading up?'

If he'd been wearing anything other than just shorts he might have had a chance of hiding the flush of embarrassment he could feel blooming in his body. Lea's eye drifted to his throat where the heat gathered.

'Oh. You have?' Her eyes snapped back up to his and a beautiful, gentle smile birthed on her face. 'Thank you, Reilly.'

His insides turned to mush. She could play him so easily. Still…

'Will you stay, Lea? Just until the baby is born and Molly is well?' If she noticed he'd just extended the timeframe, she didn't question it.

Which was just as well, because he didn't fully understand it himself.

CHAPTER EIGHT

'WELCOME to Minamurra.'

Reilly took her hand as Lea scrambled out of her car, and she tugged it away ungraciously. She'd just spent three hours lecturing herself on all the reasons spending too much time with him would be a bad idea and he'd near undone it with one touch.

'Thanks for coming, Lea.'

'No worries. Yurraji was too quiet after you and your travelling band of ponies shipped out anyway.'

She didn't tell him the past two days had reminded her of the quiet at Jarndirri when Anna and Sapphie hadn't been there, when it had just been she and her father rattling around the enormous homestead not saying a word to each other.

If you can't say something nice...

She solved her proximity problem by twisting away to look at God's Gift spooking around the paddock, forcing Reilly to drop the hand that was still in his. 'How is he? Better?'

Reilly turned to face the same way. 'I was hoping you being here might tip the familiarity balance. He likes you.'

At least someone did! 'And if it doesn't?' She couldn't look at him. The answer to this question said a lot about the type of man he was.

He blew air through tight lips. 'If he doesn't, he goes back to his mob. He's no use to me like this.'

Lea nodded slowly, disguising her relief. Good answer.
Good man.

She shushed her subconscious and let an excited Molly out of her safety seat to immediately run off in search of Max the Cat.

'Walk!' Lea called after her before easing her way down the grassed slope of the homestead towards the paddock holding the three wild horses. She took the chance to have a proper look around, to notice the things she'd been too nervous and then too upset to appreciate during her last visit.

'My father would have loved Minamurra.' She stunned herself as much as Reilly with her unplanned confession. Her father was the last person she'd ever think to discuss publicly. Reilly caught up and walked beside her, a tiny bit too close for comfort. She hurried on, uncomfortable, suddenly, looking about. 'Well-planned layout, a shed for every machine. Nice and linear. The kind of meticulous order he liked around him.'

He looked at her as if recognising something for the first time. 'That must have been tough to grow up with. Children being the natural enemy of order, I mean.'

Lea chuckled, knowing how true that was with Molly, and how much she appreciated order herself. Then she frowned. How had she forgotten that she and her father had that in common?

'I guess I learned it somewhere. Shame he never lived to see the miracle.' Her frown deepened. Would they have found more common ground as they both got older? Clashed less as life forced them both to compromise?

Maybe she should have just smiled and nodded, said that any of her father's dozen ludicrous plans for improving the station were a terrific idea. Or told him that she didn't care about the welfare of the strapling calves in the dehorning yard. Or said she'd never seen him having sex with their summer cook in the dead of night—while her mother had lain dying just rooms away.

Perhaps honesty wasn't all it was made out to be.

The mares approached immediately, moving straight to Reilly and nosing him for treats, ever ready to bolt off at the first sign of trouble. The stallion kept a wary distance, but stopped jogging when he saw Lea. She hoisted herself up onto the first timber-fence rail and leaned towards him, cooing. Reilly kept the mares occupied off to one side but watched the proceedings intently. The stallion turned towards her voice, no more, and gave a full-body shudder. He looked plain relieved.

'I'll be damned,' Reilly muttered.

'It worked?' Lea was as surprised as he sounded. The stallion stood placidly, for a wild brumby.

'That's the first time in two days he's not been clawing up my training paddock. Yeah, I'd say it worked.'

Their eyes connected over the top of Golden Girl's golden mane. Reilly looked impressed, and somewhat confused. It felt too good standing here next to him, suddenly valuable for something. Appreciated.

She willed herself not to enjoy it. 'So now what?'

'Now there's two of us glad to have you here.'

Reilly gave her the room that opened out onto the wide veranda surrounding the house. The room furthest from his.

Message sent and received. Still, it wasn't entirely without redeeming qualities. It looked out onto a wetland area behind the house, a dam-fed pond covered in water lilies with vibrant, purple-and-yellow blooms soaking up the sun's rays. A dozen water-birds picked through the reeds lining its banks and dragonflies caused the only disturbance on its glassy surface.

Beautiful. Very Kimberley.

'This is lovely, thank you.'

Standing there with Reilly only made her think of the last time they'd been in a bedroom together. Her body temperature shot up three degrees at the memory. She shook it off. If they were going to see each other every day, share a house, she had to get a handle on these crazy emotions.

He cleared his throat. 'I've put Molly in here with you for the first few nights, but there's a nice room all set up for her next door. Move her in whenever she's ready.' He pulled a mattress out from under her bed, and Lea forced herself to stand motionless.

It would take no effort at all to just nudge him...

She slapped herself mentally. 'Uh... Are you okay if we take a few minutes to unpack? Is there anything you need me to do first?'

Surprise had him straightening. 'You're a guest here, Lea. You don't have to do anything.'

'I'm going to need to do something; I'll go spare otherwise.'

'We'll figure something out. What are you good at?'

She laughed. 'Riding.'

'Hmm. That won't be happening. This whole thing is an exercise in safety.'

Her heart dropped; as if she needed the reminder. This was all about Molly and the unborn baby. She shook her head. It was as it should be. She'd been foolish never to let herself think about what a bad combination a sickening Molly and impassable roads would be. Or the risk to the cells she carried if something went wrong. Reilly had offered an olive branch decorated with a great big common-sense ribbon. His airstrip was set up for the outback Flying Doctor service; he even had his own light plane if it came to that. He had staff, mountains of food and an enormous empty house where she and Molly could have their own private space. And he was on the good side of the highway that flooded every wet season.

Lea had only had the lumpy, questionable warmth of her Curran pride.

It hadn't been enough to risk her daughter's future for.

'Coming here is not something I'm particularly comfortable with, Reilly. But I've already made enough decisions based on what I need. It's taken me over five years to work it out, but I know that now. I won't be taking any unnecessary risks.'

Her deep, enduring loneliness had never been the right reason to have a child. Nor her all-consuming hunger to be a mother. But what about making a new child…? She caught herself stroking her swollen stomach again and forced her hand away.

She was bonding with this baby. That was not good. She didn't know this child yet. She felt it, yes, but she didn't *know* it. As hard as it would be, handing it to Reilly would still be easier than watching Molly die a painful, slow death. Knowing it was loved and safe and would have a good life with a good man…

She lifted her eyes to his and realised he *was* a good man. A man who just desperately wanted to be a parent. Just as she had.

He yielded under her intense regard. 'Why don't you both rest for a bit?' he said, shuffling to his feet. 'You can unpack later on.'

After packing all morning and a three-hour drive, exhaustion dogged her heels, despite her best attempts at keeping it at bay: pregnancy trade-off number one. Lea missed having the stamina of her youth—heck, of last year! She rubbed her neck.

'That sounds heavenly,' she said. 'Making fingers and earlobes sure takes a lot out of a person. I have no idea how mum did it while…'

She practically gasped at what she'd been about to say. Reilly finished for her.

'While she was pregnant with you?'

Lea swallowed. She'd never spoken of this to anyone. She shook her head. Flicked her eyes to his. 'My sister. Mum was pregnant with Anna when her breast cancer was diagnosed. I don't know how she did it, considering what carrying a child takes out of you when you're healthy.'

His dark eyes were bottomless and entirely compassionate. 'She must have been a strong woman—to go through with the pregnancy, knowing she'd never get to see the child grow up.' He reeled back, maybe realising what he was about to say.

And to whom.

'It's okay, Reilly. It helps keep it in perspective. All I have to worry about is being left alone myself. Mum had to leave two tiny daughters in the care of a faithless husband.'

Reilly's head dropped. 'Your father cheated on your mother?' Lea nodded. 'And she knew?'

'How could she not? It happened in the kitchen just metres from her room.'

Reilly swore. 'How do you know?'

Lea sank onto the bed, staring out at the purple blanket of flowers on the pond. 'They weren't very quiet. I got up. I was too young to understand what I was seeing. But I got more than an academic education at boarding school, and I heard things over giggled conversations that put it all into heart-breaking context.' She took a deep breath. 'It was the night Sapphie was conceived.'

The silence was massively telling. 'But you're close to your half-sister, regardless?'

She shrugged. 'Sins of the father and all that. I grew up with Sapphie. I loved her as a friend long before I knew she was a Curran.' *Even longer before everyone else knew.* 'I felt dirty for years, holding onto that secret. As though suspecting made me somehow a terrible friend.'

A worse daughter.

'Did you tell your father?'

'God, no! That nasty little secret festered into a soul-sore until the day it just burst from my lips—that I knew what he'd done while my mother lay dying two rooms away.'

He had not looked her in the eye since.

'No wonder the two of you had a difficult relationship,' Reilly said.

'We never recovered. I didn't want to. What kind of a man would *do* that?'

Reilly sank down onto the bed across from her. 'A weak, frightened one? Desperate to make the pain stop just for a moment?'

Lea stared razor blades at him. 'Are you defending him?'

He raised both hands. 'Ah, no. That would be suicidal. Was the question rhetorical?'

Her chest heaved. She pressed her lips together. 'No. I would like to understand. Would you do it?' she whispered. 'You're a man.'

'I'd like to say I wouldn't.' His warm eyes held hers. 'But until I'm in his position, watching my wife die by degrees, I can only speculate.' He shook his head. 'Did he love your mother?'

She shrugged. 'He said he did.'

'Maybe the chance of just a few minutes of comfort and oblivion in the arms of an eager, living woman was too strong? Maybe he couldn't be strong for everyone.'

Lea stared, closer to understanding just how flawed, how human, her father was than ever before.

'I think we're all capable of doing things out of character when we're desperate,' Reilly continued.

Wasn't that the truth?

'Things we might not be proud of later.'

The tone of his voice drew her eyes to his in time to catch the dying flash of something indefinable. Regret? Sorrow?

Molly-of-the-impeccable-timing came scuffing into the room just then, and Reilly seemed suddenly to realise he was sitting on a bed with Lea. He leapt to his feet. 'I'll leave you to your unpacking. I have a few things to be doing outside. See you later, Lea. Night, Molly.'

Then he was gone.

Lea helped Molly change the sheets on her mattress to her favourite ones with puppies on them and then slipped her into her pyjamas. She tucked her heavy-eyed daughter into bed unbathed, and she was asleep before Lea had even unpacked one suitcase.

She thought about her mother as she started on the second case. Had she felt this same bone-deep despair at the thought of never seeing Lea growing up, of leaving her alone? Karen Curran must have had much more personal strength than her eldest daughter.

Everyone seemed to have more personal strength than her. Look at what Anna had been through. Sapphie, too. Even Jared.

Jared's strength, after everything he had been through, was what she modelled herself on for years afterwards. Because of him, she went back to school with renewed purpose and graduated with honours. But her father even managed to ruin that by trying to palm her off on Jared to get him to stay on Jarndirri, like some kind of twisted mail-order bride. Things had got horribly awkward between them then, so she'd taken herself and her online university-course to live with her maternal grandfather in Parker Ridge. Far away from her father.

He'd practically packed for her.

Her chest ached at the irony as she slipped the last of her clothes into the giant chest of drawers. Here she was, unpacking that very same suitcase in Reilly Martin's house—the father of the child she'd created the day her own father had been buried.

Was that some weird kind of cosmic wheel? Going over and over the past sure wasn't changing the future. It wasn't helping her to move forward. Maybe it was time to do something differently.

Exhaustion dogged her. The smell of horses and fresh straw wafted in on the warm evening breeze. Reilly's effective aircon was uncomfortably cool to her, after years of slugging it out naturally. She crawled up onto the bed and pulled the light sheet up over her body, tucking her hands around her emerging belly, her eyes slowly losing focus in the sea of green and purple outside her window.

One by one, the sounds of the day dropped off until the only thing she could hear was the drone of distant insects, and even those seemed to merge, as she slipped into dream, into the thrum-thrum of a tiny heartbeat.

Reilly stood on the veranda and stared through the open doorway at the woman within. She'd slept so long, he'd felt compelled to come and check that she was breathing. She was; the same deep, slow breath of the frogs that slowed their metabolism so they could ride out the blistering summer deep below the baked earth.

This little frog wasn't waking until morning. And Molly was zonked out next to her, draped in pretty puppy-sheets that Lea must have brought with her from home. For Molly, a dusk bedtime was normal.

Lea, not so much. Shouldn't she eat something? If her body had thought food was more important than rest right now it would probably have woken her up. Wouldn't it? He glanced sideways at the darkened doorway.

Watching her was like looking on Sleeping Beauty frozen in time, locked in her glass case for eternity. It was only the fairy-tale image that lessened the creep factor he felt standing in the shadows of her doorway, staring.

He'd not handled himself well the other day. Inviting her to stay—his lips twisted at the word 'inviting'—had been a spontaneous and completely un-thought-through piece of Martin brilliance. In that moment, it had seemed like the best idea in the world, because in that moment his hormones had still been ruling play.

That much he understood. It was the deeper connotations that had him frowning.

Now he stood gazing on her sleeping form like it was some kind of holy relic. Drawing peace from her serene expression, from the way her hands still curved protectively around her belly. The softness of her lips that parted as though on a sigh. Fearing how badly he wanted to touch them again.

His fingers burned with the need.

What the blazes was wrong with him? One minute he wanted to shake her, the next he was fantasising about her lips. His emotions were like a bull ride.

Enough.

He stepped in from the veranda and reached around to close the two sleeping beauties behind glass double-doors for the night, and as he did one of the hinges protested loudly.

'Reilly?'

He froze where he stood then turned slowly, his heart thumping. Lea was still asleep, murmuring. Murmuring *his name* in her sleep. It shot straight to his gut—south of his gut, actually.

'It's okay, Lea. Sleep now.' His own voice was thick and low. And enormously strained. 'I'll see you in the morning.'

She made an indecipherable sound and let herself tumble back into oblivion. He pulled the curtains across and locked the doors behind him, sending Lea and Molly into complete darkness. Then he turned back to the light of the veranda, leaned back against the wall and finally released his breath.

His heart beat so hard, it ached...

It didn't take a psychology degree to understand what was going on here. His body was responding to a range of instinctive cues as ancient as the granite ridges surrounding them. Answering the glowing fertility of hers. Animal attraction, pure and simple.

It was the dying days of the dry season, the land all around him was building up to the wet, the most abundant, verdant time of the year. The time when waterholes swelled, enthusiastic amphibians burst from their underground burrows and wildlife started pairing up so that their offspring emerged just as the new, sweet grasses did.

Sex was going on all around him. Everywhere.

And he hadn't been with anyone for months—more than months. Since his diagnosis. But Lea Curran wasn't his usual type. He liked women blonde, eager and available. Not prickly, brunette...and pregnant.

He marched off down the veranda back towards the front door. Maybe that was it—pure biology? She was already pregnant, she represented no biological risk whatsoever. But she did represent what he'd only just accepted he'd never have—a female large with his child.

And that was disturbingly seductive. No matter what his head said.

Two hours later, he was rattling around alone in the main part of the silent homestead as always. The sprawling house was designed to take a large family without popping a seam. Pity it had never had more than three people in it at one time.

And likely never would. It would be just him and the baby. And Mrs Dawes, who'd been the housekeeper since he was tiny.

Holding out for the right woman seemed pointless when he had nothing but a big, empty house and roomfuls of other people's antiques to offer a woman. The kind of woman he wished for would go elsewhere, to a man who could offer children. Family.

It had been years since he'd last been truly attracted to the women he slept with. Had felt the kind of interest that lasted longer than an evening. The kind of interest that built anticipation like the onset of the wet season, and then wasn't fully released by the first downpour.

Nearly six years, if he was counting. The weekend Molly was conceived.

He finally let himself go right back into the seductive, taboo detail. Repeatedly. Knowing he'd fathered a child with Lea gave the memories a primal kind of resonance. Caveman Reilly showed his face again. He imagined himself buried to the hilt inside all that fertility, creating their new child, his genes multiplying radically in her belly through more traditional means.

His groan was a tortured mix of regret and passion and it was all he could do not to take himself back to Lea's bedroom door.

But that was just lust talking. Welcome, definitely; it was a timely validation that fertility was the only function he'd lost. If his body's reaction to Lea's ample charms was any indication, it was more than ready for a road test, evidence that he was half a man, at least. Staring down the barrel of forty years of emptiness, wandering around the house dwelling on the family he'd never have—it was hardly the stuff libido was made of. Reilly Martin didn't do emptiness well. He'd made a specialty of filling the empty places.

He glanced at the cupboard above the microwave where he knew Mrs Dawes kept a bottle of cooking spirits. It was the only alcohol he allowed in the house. And it bothered the heck out of him that he knew exactly where she kept it.

'Hey.' The soft voice came from behind him.

Reilly spun as though she'd caught him cracking the top on the bottle. She was fresh from waking, a crease still marking her sleep-flushed cheek, looking more relaxed and at ease than he'd ever seen her. Except when she'd run with the brumbies that time.

That Lea made him think of tangled sheets and tongues. This Lea was almost childlike.

'Did I miss dinner?'

She was hungry. He knew it. 'I figured you needed sleep more than supper.'

'I think I did. But now I'm ready to eat one of your horses. Do you mind if I make myself something?'

Visions of cooking spirits evaporated on his chuckle. 'If it protects the livestock, help yourself.'

She ate like she rode, full throttle. Unapologetic. Watching her polish off Mrs Dawes' leftover steak-and-kidney pie was like watching locusts swarm. Even for a countrywoman she had a healthy appetite.

'Is that you or…?' At her questioning look, he nodded from her empty plate to her belly.

She grinned and stretched back, satiated. 'Would it be wrong to blame the pregnancy?'

The silence that fell didn't feel awkward.

'Tell me about Anna,' he surprised himself by asking. Getting to know her better hadn't been on his radar when he'd pressured her into staying at Minamurra. 'What's she like?'

'Everyone loves Anna.'

'Not what I asked.'

Lea sighed. 'She's the perfect outback wife: smart, loyal, determined. She and her husband Jared make a good pair.'

'I sense some history here.' It wasn't a question. Dark eyes regarded her steadily.

Lea pushed away from the table and loaded her dish and cutlery into the dishwasher before crossing to the polished kettle sitting on the hob. One quick button-press had the flame magically popping into life. She turned back into the patient silence and waved her hand dismissively. 'I was the oldest, so sometimes Anna and I clashed. You know siblings…there's always history.'

'Nope, can't say I do. I'm a Martin original.'

Said with levity but hiding such sadness. 'Take it as read that there's always baggage between siblings, especially sisters. It doesn't mean we love each other any less. There's nothing Anna wouldn't do for me. And vice versa. Sapphie too.'

He watched her long and hard before finally speaking. 'That's nice. Special.'

The stare went on just long enough to bring her tiny neck-hairs to attention. For Lea it just *was*. She couldn't imagine not having Anna or Sapphie—or Jared and Liam, for that matter— a phone call away.

Time this conversation turned two-way.

'You were an only child?' she asked.

'I was. Childbearing was not something my mother wanted to do again once she got over the novelty factor.'

Lea polished her hand over her tummy, knowing how wonderful her first pregnancy had been for her. Despite the aches and the sickness and the tiredness. 'I'm sorry.'

'Why? I had it great. Fantastic property. Famous parents. Everything money could buy.'

She remembered what he'd said at the waterhole. 'And no one to share it with.'

Reilly laughed, a harsh, unforgiving kind of sound. 'As it happens, I don't play well with others.'

Lea felt compelled to say something. 'I'm sure that's not true.' Although she was very sure it was. Suddenly a familiar sensation drew her focus down to her body. Her hand followed her gaze.

'You're smiling?'

Her head snapped back up. 'I'm sorry. It's…' She smiled again, completely unable not to as joy filled her. 'It moves sometimes, when I'm not expecting it. I've only just started to feel movement. I was beginning to worry.'

Worry? Now why had she told him that?

He was on his feet in an instant, crossing to her with a fierce scowl on his handsome face. 'What kind of movement?'

'The best kind. The kind that just says, "Hey, I'm here".'

An intense focus sharpened his expression. She forgot he had a professional interest in pregnancy, but had very little opportunity to ask his equine mothers what it felt like.

'Do you… Would you like me to describe it?'

'Can you? I mean, will that be difficult for you?'

Probably, given that she tried to not think about it at all. But the deep longing that glowed in his eyes was added incentive. She wanted to give him this, even if it meant opening the emotional box she'd sealed shut. She slid both hands under her T-shirt to frame the slightly hardened roundness. She hadn't really thought about how to describe it before. She closed her eyes a moment to get it right. 'It's like…ripples. Deep inside. Some people feel it as butterflies, but for me it's kind of a tide. A pulling. I know it's shifting. Maybe that causes the fluid to swirl.'

'Do you feel it on the outside?'

She lifted her lashes. His gaze was fixated on where her hands rubbed over her stomach.

He really is interested. As unexpected as that was, she felt no reason to hold the knowledge to herself. She'd been doing that so long, the chance to share it with someone, anyone, was enticing. Even if he was the last man on the planet she'd have expected to be sharing with. The only man on the planet who had the right.

She took a breath. 'Sometimes. Would you like to feel?'

He just about stumbled over the kitchen chair in his haste to back off. But he pulled up on the other side of it and watched avidly.

'Come on, Reilly. You've already compared me to one of your horses. Just pretend I'm on all fours and wearing a bridle.'

The heat that flared in his eyes then had nothing to do with embarrassment, and it was Lea's turn to blush. That expression was more the Reilly she expected. She'd been seeing less of him, lately, and more of his quiet, sensitive twin. She stepped towards him; he stiffened immediately. There was the slightest power rush in watching his reaction to her advancing body. Big, bad Reilly Martin was nervous.

Because of her.

'Just one feel.' She spoke to him like he spoke to God's Gift: confident; soothing. She took his left hand and placed it surely onto her skin near where she could still feel some residual activity. Her warm skin blazed with remembrance at his touch. Five years had done nothing to dilute her flesh's memory. His fingers were large and just slightly work-roughened and Lea had to clamp her jaw to prevent the sensation of pleasure.

Just man hands; nothing special.

She shifted his fingers like a stethoscope, closer to one hip. 'Can you feel anything?' Her question was more of a breath. Her eyes darted up to his, where they locked on what his fingers were doing.

He shook his head, so close to hers.

Damn. She was suddenly burning for someone else to feel it, to make this all real. She shifted his hand lower, into the curve of her pelvis.

His eyes widened, met hers. 'Was that the baby?'

She laughed. 'I don't know. What did it feel like?'

'A hand waving.'

She closed her fingers over his consolingly. 'No; it's still too small. That might have been the fluttering?'

And with her disappointing words the magic of the moment evaporated, leaving a man and a woman in a kitchen, with his big man-hands closer to her panty line than anyone had been in years. In fact, the last hands had been his, too.

His eyes locked on hers; his thumb slid tenderly across her hip. She drowned in their intensity.

God, Lea. What are you doing?

She shifted sideways out of his reach, striving for casualness. Her suddenly rapid heartbeat thumped out through her laugh. 'So, similar to horses after all?'

He didn't answer directly, but he stepped back and gave her the space she needed. 'Horses. Humans. Either way, it's a miracle.'

She stared at him. 'I imagine this is not something you expected would ever happen in your life?'

His laugh was bitter. 'Not exactly.'

'Were you planning a family before it happened?'

'It?'

His glower and single arched eyebrow didn't frighten her off. Not this time. 'Before your injuries.'

'Did I have plans for a loving wife and a house full of kids?' He had to think about it. 'Not consciously, but, yeah. I always imagined myself sharing this place with someone. Handing it over to someone when I got old.'

His pain was visible. 'I'm so sorry.'

'Why? You didn't cause the damage. Rodeo was my choice. Besides, as it turns out, I have a child and a second one on the way. That's a heck of a lot more than I was expecting out of life. I think I can survive not having the loving wife to come home to.'

Lea's eyes fell away. What would that be like, coming home to this man? Being loved by him? His body heat seemed to reach out to her.

Conversation…conversation… She cleared her throat. 'So, how long has Mrs Dawes worked here?'

He leaned casually onto the kitchen table, crossing his

booted feet. 'My whole life. She and her husband were hired when my parents bought Minamurra.'

'Did I meet her husband?'

Reilly shook his dark head. 'He lives out with the ringers.'

That got her attention. 'Isn't that a bit…unconventional?'

He smiled, the first look of affection she'd seen him give for anything other than a horse. And Molly. 'This coming from you?' He chuckled. 'I think it keeps the romance alive for them. They sneak around like clandestine lovers to spend time together, and when they're not they have their own space, their own interests. Plus, I'm not convinced they're actually married.'

'Really? How scandalous. Good on you, Mrs Dawes.' Her laugh was too loud for the quiet kitchen.

Reilly suddenly realised how few laughs this whole house had absorbed into its serious walls. 'You don't mind a bit of scandal?'

She sat in the chair closest to his crossed legs and tipped her head up to him. 'Not if it paves the way for true love.'

'You don't strike me as someone who'd put much stock in true love.'

Lea's face shuttered over. 'Really? Why's that?'

'I had you pegged more as a "love the one you're with" type.'

Her eyes darkened. 'Appearances can be deceptive. But, as it happens, that's what I had you pegged as.'

'You'd be right.' *To a point.*

'So, tell me about your first love,' she asked.

Whoa. Unexpected turn, and no good way to answer that. 'I have. Grita, the Swedish backpacker.'

She rolled her eyes. 'First *love*, Reilly, not first lover.'

'There's a difference?' He knew that would earn him one of her tight smiles. 'Why so interested?'

'I'm not interested.' Colour streaked up the ridge of her cheekbone. It suited her. 'We're going to be in each other's lives for months. I thought we could get to know each other a little bit. You know…pass the time.'

It was too easy to slip back when she kept handing him openings like that. 'I can think of better ways of passing the time…'

Her eyes glittered. 'No doubt. But, as we've established, I'm over four months' pregnant.'

She thought that was the slightest deterrent? It only made her more attractive.

Her pink lips twisted and she changed tack. 'Okay, first kiss, then.'

If not for her determined expression—that face said conversation-or-death—he'd think she was working up to a proposition. Who talked first kisses with a man they had once slept with? Near midnight. Alone in the middle of nowhere.

Lea Curran did, apparently.

He smiled and shuffled his feet so the other one was on top. 'Same answer, as it happens. Grita was a great few weeks.'

She tossed her head and went to stand. 'Okay, forget it—'

He met her on her feet and pushed her by the shoulders gently back down into the seat, taking the opportunity to sink back down onto the table edge much closer than before. 'This conversation was your idea, there's no bailing now. What about you? First kiss.'

She glared up at him. Almost didn't answer. 'Jared.'

His stomach hit the floor. 'You shared your first kiss with Jared? As in, your brother-in-law?'

Her chin lifted. 'Get your mind out of the gutter, Martin. We were sixteen. Friends. Curious. He was pretty much the only decent boy my age for two-hundred kilometres.'

'How was it?' A question like that should have earned him a slap. But there was something about this night, this conversation.

'With Jared?' She smiled. 'Wet. Gross. Pretty sure he agreed. I gather my sister's a better kisser.'

Hard to imagine. He still remembered the shape of her mouth from those years ago. He swallowed hard. 'I wouldn't take it personally. Kissing's all about science.'

She snorted. 'Science? Not very romantic.'

He slid an inch closer. Their bodies were almost touching, the heat from his extended legs merging with the kiln of her body. A body burning from more than just incubating a baby, if he wasn't mistaken.

'Kisses aren't about romance,' he said, 'They're about sex. A good kiss is about chemistry. Or don't you remember?'

Her voice dropped slightly, and the blaze in her eyes told him she remembered very well. Was she thinking about that motel? He certainly was. There'd been a lot of kissing then, bold, brave kisses. But nothing like the chemistry pinging between them now. Yet they weren't even touching. This woman should come with a caution sign for the residual current running through her.

His entire lower half pulsed erotically in synch.

'I beg to differ,' she said softly, exciting his body with promise. 'A good kiss is about timing, anticipation, connection.'

He bent forward, closer to her face. 'Show me.' Her pupils widened, marginalising the flecks of green, blue and brown to the very rims of her irises. But she didn't move away. 'Show me how a kiss is about more than sex.'

For the life of him, he really wanted to know.

She wavered, her enormous eyes locked fast on him, and then invisible threads lifted her face towards his. She looked one-hundred-percent woman now and completely awake. His heart started to hammer against his chest wall, wanting out.

Their entire conversation since she'd unwittingly stumbled on him in the kitchen had led to this moment. And they both knew it.

'If a kiss was just about sex…' Lea breathed the words against his lips, tipping her face so that her forehead almost rested against his, a sweet, trusting little move that roused every primal instinct lurking deep in his body. 'Then we'd be kissing now.'

Reilly snatched forward with his lips to prove his point. She avoided him with a quick twist that put her mouth perilously close to his throat. His ear. Awareness shivered down his neck as her hot breath danced around him. Her hair brushed against his hypersensitive flesh.

'But what makes a kiss romantic, about so much more than sex…' she drew his face like a magnet, curling towards those pink, ripe lips '…is the question mark. How will it taste?' She rubbed his stubbled cheek with her own soft one, dragging the corner of that delicious mouth closer to his. 'How will it feel?'

His eyes fluttered shut as she traced the lids lightly with her lips.

God above, she was going to kill him. Five-year-old memories surged around the room, practically crashing into the furniture. His mouth was at once dry with anticipation and wet with desire as her lips returned to hover just millimetres from his.

'And, most importantly…' She raised smoky eyes, a tiny smile shaping her mouth. Her hands were braced either side of his hips on the kitchen table and he closed his eyes as she leaned that final inch forward. *Thank God.* 'How will I possibly survive never knowing?'

She pushed herself to her feet and away from him, and crossed back to the hob to see to the bubbling kettle. His eyes opened in disbelief, his body screaming with the denial. 'Never knowing' was no longer an option.

And it had nothing to do with romance.

Lea gasped as strong, masculine hands spun her back just as the simmering kettle started to sing. Its mounting pitch matched her fever exactly. Reilly folded her into strong arms and tipped her half off her feet before she could even suck in a breath to protest. Her hard, pregnant midsection pressed against his hard, flat one.

His blazing mouth—soft and powerful, familiar and new—slid over hers, demanding a response she was gasping to give. Hot and wet and urgent. Exactly as she'd remembered in her dreams. Her little lesson in romance had sapped her of resistance, and she literally panted for a kissing lesson from someone she was fast considering to be the sexiest man alive.

Never mind that he held such a low opinion of her; he kissed like a god. Her breath ached in her tight, trembling chest.

He consumed her, feasting on her lips and pressing her body perfectly into his, his tongue burning the inner reaches of the mouth she helplessly opened to him. The heady lip-work seemed to strengthen him everywhere she was weakening, and he held her up as her legs gave out.

The oxygen that should have been surging through her body

pooled into her core, prioritising her vital organs as though her life was in danger.

In danger of being kissed out of her, perhaps.

The kettle was piping now, spewing steam out of its angry top and forming a layer of sweat on the overhead cabinets that rivalled the rapidly forming dampness on her own skin. Some desperate, distant part of her consciousness ordered her hands to remain clenched, not to join the fray. But the roaring thunder of her blood drowned out the request, and her hands did what she suddenly realised she'd wanted to do since that first day at Yurraji. They fought their way under the layers of his clothing and spread out against the furnace of his muscular back.

She knew those muscles like Braille. Every dip. Every rise. Every sinew.

God, how she'd missed them.

Her mind screamed a protest at her body but it came out as a choked mix of fury, frustration and desire. Reilly must have felt it more than heard it over the protesting kettle, but he righted her up onto her feet and let his hands slip up into her hair. Her shirt rode up against him as she swayed to her feet, and she realised she was stretching up to prevent their lips from breaking apart.

She was kissing *him*.

He closed his fists in her hair and gentled his mouth. Slower, wetter, more rubbing, more heavy breathing. Lea rubbed her body against his as the kettle kept up its piercing aria. Undeniable, one-hundred-proof *sex*.

The man had made his point.

She pushed away, gasping and dragging her wrist across her throbbing mouth. With trembling hands she turned and put the kettle out of its misery, and the ear-splitting crescendo died away instantly.

In the new silence, her chest heaved. His chest heaved. Tortured breathing filled the air. It was a tiny comfort that Reilly looked as stunned as she felt. His molten eyes assessed her warily as she backed towards the door. But he didn't stop her leaving.

'I'm just… I think I'll… Bed.' Words just would not form on her swollen lips. 'Alone,' she added hastily as a dangerous gleam sparked in his eyes.

Again, silence.

She turned and wobbled to the doorway on jelly legs. But as she disappeared through it she heard Reilly's voice as he cursed, thick and low.

CHAPTER NINE

THE more she learned, the stranger it became. There was no end to the ramifications of her decision to create a life that could also save Molly's. For example, learning that her daughter's blood type would eventually change to match the baby's.

Lea shook her head, frowning. 'Did you know that Molly will end up with two types of DNA? Her flesh will be her own but her blood will match the new baby's.'

Reilly looked up from a sheath of accounts spread across his desk and considered that. He wasn't startled enough; it must have already occurred to him. 'Handy if she wants to become an arch criminal, I guess.'

Lea chuckled and conceded the point from her comfortable position on the sofa. Molly slept stretched out the length of it with her head on Lea's rapidly diminishing lap as the rain drummed hypnotically on Minamurra's tin roof.

It felt like it had been raining the best part of the month.

She sobered. 'The more I learn, the more I realise how many lives could be affected by this decision.'

Reilly glanced back up at her, leaving his figures again. 'You hadn't thought about all of that?'

She'd never been much good at hiding her blushes and one broke free right now. 'I... Yes, of course. But I hadn't... The long-term implications weren't...' She took a deep breath, then looked at Molly. Then back at Reilly. She sighed. 'Actually, no. At least, not for long. I figured that all of those things would be surmountable. None of them had much impact against the chance to save Molly's life.'

He regarded her steadily. She held her breath. This was where the inevitable criticism would come, the preaching and speechifying, Bryce Curran style.

He lowered his eyes carefully back to his desk. 'Gotta say, I'd just be happy to make some impact on this spreadsheet.'

Lea blinked. 'That's it—no sermon? You don't have an opinion to share about how irresponsible that was? How I should have thought about it longer? How careless I've been?'

He looked back up and shrugged. 'I'm sure you don't need my condemnation stacking up on top of your own.'

Lea drew in a tight breath. He was right.

'Why the frown?' he asked.

Lea forced the furrows away and answered carefully. 'I'm more used to people using the ammunition I give them.'

He lowered the spreadsheet to the desk. 'Someone else might have lied about not having given the ramifications due thought. Covered their butt.'

Her answer was simple. 'I don't lie.' She'd made some bad choices in her life, but she'd lasted thirty years without letting a lie knowingly cross her lips. She wasn't about to start now. 'It was the last thing my mother asked of me.' The only thing she'd asked.

Let no lie into your heart, baby girl.

Reilly's eyes went straight to Molly. He was right; she'd been Molly's age at the time. Her heart squeezed, imagining for one moment that Molly might go through what she had. Watching her mother just waste away. Begging her—literally, on her tiny, scabbed knees—not to go. That she'd be a good girl. A *better* girl. Her tiny heart fracturing.

Lea's throat thickened now and her hand tightened in her daughter's hair.

'You've kept that pledge your whole life?' His voice was gentle. 'I'm sure that's not what she would have wanted.'

'No. But it's something I could do. For her.' She sucked back the sting of tears and met Reilly's eyes again. 'It became a habit.

And then an obsession. It was so hard at times—at school, with my sisters, my father. I feel like going back on it now would make all of that pain worthless.'

The clock ticked quietly. 'So I could ask you anything and you'd have to tell me the truth?'

'Not *have* to. Choose to, yes.' She glared at him warily. Necessity had forced her to become queen of the loophole: it wasn't a lie if you didn't answer. It wasn't a lie if you talked around it. It wasn't a lie if you tackled a question with another question.

Deflection. Avoidance. Fast talking.

Reilly nodded, then went back to his spreadsheet.

Lea's heart thundered. 'Aren't you going to ask me something?' His eyes lifted back to hers. 'You look like you're burning to.'

He stared at her hard. The room lost some of its air. 'I want to know a lot of things about you, Lea Curran. But I figure it's like gentling a horse; just because I *can* force it to my will doesn't mean I want to. I figure you'll tell me when you're ready.'

When—not if. Reilly could have taken her bared throat and sliced her to ribbons, but he hadn't.

He dropped his lashes for a moment then lifted them again, his eyes blazing, his voice a kiss. 'I tried to find you.'

She sucked in a breath.

'I'd almost convinced myself that you were a figment of my imagination. If not for a few of my mates who'd seen us leave the pub together, if not for the significant muscle-strain from our…marathon, you might have been a dream.'

They'd spoken before of that night but not like this. Never as though it had been a good thing.

'I couldn't believe in a community as small and fragmented as ours that I couldn't find one woman. I had a handful of facts and a physical description, and I traipsed around town like Prince Charming with the glass slipper, but no one from the district knew you. I ended up thinking you were a tourist from the Eastern States. And all along you were right round the corner.'

In the sparsely populated Kimberley, three hours away was.

Lea sat up straighter and stroked Molly's hair reassuringly. 'I didn't want to be found. I never meant to tell you anything about me at all that night. But you were easy to talk to. You listened. You seemed to understand.'

His smile had her heart flipping. 'I had incentive. The longer I kept you talking, the longer you would stay.'

A complicated silence fell on the toasty little room. Lea cleared her throat.

'I'm sorry I left like that.'

His smile was wry. 'I understand now. And it turned out to be good for me—a lesson of sorts.'

'That's very zen of you.'

Reilly chuckled. 'Seriously. A taste of my own medicine. You were exactly as anonymous as I usually liked women. But not being able to find you when I wanted to was very irritating. And the way you left...' He sighed. 'I'd done that myself on occasion. It wasn't fun.'

Lea blushed. 'You can't say I wasn't memorable, then.'

His eyes grew serious. Darker. 'Lea, that's the least of the reasons you were memorable.' He glanced back down briefly. 'Knowing you as I do now, I can see how out of character that night must have been for you. Why you might have crept out at first light.'

Accord. She'd not expected to have that between them.

She cleared her throat, dropped her eyes to the pile of papers under his fingers. 'Would you like some help with your books?' His eyebrows lifted and her hackles twitched, ready to spring into action. 'Are you more surprised I'm offering to help you or that I can count?'

Laughter rumbled through the room like the thunder that rolled across the horizon; it skirted the edges of her skin and left raised hairs in its wake. 'You didn't strike me as a numbers girl,' he said.

She frowned. 'Who do you think does all my finances? Did you notice a team of assistants littering Yurraji?'

He let the papers drop to the table. 'You mentioned a stockbroker.'

'To broker my share-trading. I manage the portfolio. I do the accounting.' Had he never noticed the commerce degree framed on her wall? What did he think she'd filled the years between school and Molly with?

'You? You track the stock exchange?'

She dropped her magazine to the floor on a soft exclamation, conscious of the sleeping child on her lap. 'You are the father of at least one girl, Reilly. You're going to have to become accustomed to females being able to do things.' The spectre of Bryce Curran shivered through the room. 'I fully expect you to doubt every part of *my* capacity, but I hope you won't treat Molly that way. She's going to have enough self-doubt to manage.'

He finally managed to blink; he sat back in his chair and turned the spreadsheet slightly in silent invitation. Lea tucked a cushion carefully under Molly's head then padded around to Reilly's side of the desk. She stepped in next to him and rested one hand on the gorgeous mahogany desk.

She scanned the top page and then quickly reviewed the pages under it, specifically not thinking about how close she was standing to him, and how all that heat coming off his body was affecting her.

'What am I looking for?'

Reilly explained the discrepancy he was trying to locate— missing funds from a half-shipment of stock-feed. Lea located the original payment and then scanned the following figures. She settled in more comfortably next to him, slightly in front, conscious on her periphery of his eyes watching her. She sensed them travelling from her fingers that moved briskly down the rows of figures in his spreadsheet, up her arms and to her shoulders. To the curve of her ever-expanding breasts. Up to the angle of her jaw. Down to her pregnant belly.

How was a woman supposed to count with all that looking going on?

She hissed sideways at him. 'I can see you, Reilly.' She leaned further forward to block his gaze and only managed to dislodge it for a moment before it fluttered to rest on her bottom—also expanding rapidly, these days.

'Reilly…' She straightened, frowning.

His apology was the least sorry she'd ever heard. But he let his expensive chair roll back so that she could get right in between him and his computer without practically sitting in his lap. She set to work on the electronic version of the data, collecting, tagging, dragging. A couple of formulas here, a few linked fields there; nothing she wasn't used to. It was first-year accounting.

All the while she was conscious of the man behind her, probably still examining her denim-clad bottom as closely as he'd run through his figures.

'Bingo.' Her eyes narrowed just as they fell on a number that seemed suspiciously out of place in its column. The discrepancy, an error in a single formula. Reilly pushed to his feet behind her and peered over her shoulder as she highlighted the guilty cell on the screen. 'You have a one in this formula, where a point-five should be.'

This close, the clean cotton smell of him tantalised her receptors. He practically cloaked her with his body. And he knew it, guaranteed. His breath was warm against her ear as he spoke; his confusion, at least, was completely genuine.

'How did you find that?'

She couldn't turn to speak to him without ending up pressed against him, and she couldn't step away easily. Standing still was presently the best option. Never mind that it felt fabulous, like she was born to fit into his body. 'I fragmented your data, subbed it out and it was fine. It was just on this page that it went hinky. So I traced it back, and…'

She saw his face turn towards hers in the reflection of the computer monitor. Felt his words against her ear.

'You make bookkeeping sound so much better than dirty talk.'

His voice was husky and his closeness drugged her. Her eyes glanced briefly at a soundly sleeping Molly and then fluttered closed. She tipped her head imperceptibly away from him, lengthening her throat. She needed his lips there—needed, not wanted. Her body was responding in total violation of her mind.

'Shall I talk to you about vectors?' She threw the joke out

like a lifeline and then clung to it, bobbing dangerously in a tide of attraction.

Reilly chuckled again and leaned past her to alter the formula on his computer. His broad chest rubbed against her shoulder—only her shoulder—but Lea doubled her hold on that lifeline.

Breathe! In…out… 'I take it you're not so good with figures?'

'Not the mathematical kind.' His lopsided grin caused her pulse to hitch. 'I don't see the logic. I don't know most of the rules.' He studied her closely—microscope-close. She stiffened. 'Lea, would you consider doing my books while you're staying here? Maybe teach me how you work them?'

Her eyebrows plunged into a wrinkle-forming frown. 'You're asking for my help?' Admitting he wasn't good at something—the great Reilly Martin? What was she supposed to do with that? She hadn't really seen that happening in her life, and certainly hadn't expected it from him. It dawned on her that maybe he was baring his throat just a little bit too.

Just that simple act had her heart thumping. She forced it to slow. Having warm and fuzzy thoughts was not going to help her situation. She didn't want to start connecting with him. Liking him.

Needing him.

He regarded her seriously. 'I haven't built Minamurra up to this level by doing everything myself, or kidding myself that I can. I play to the strengths of my team, and right now your accounting strengths are looking pretty good to me. I'm not too proud to stand back and let you help me.'

Lea took a deep breath. She was officially out of her depth. The men she knew were all doers—obnoxious and painful with it—like her father, who believed he simply could not make a mistake. Or determined, resolute and uber-capable, like Jared.

Here was a man's man—a hundred-proof outback ringer—not only admitting he couldn't do something as well as she, but giving her the chance to run with it. Letting her have her head.

Lea took it, but not without a healthy dose of humour to shelter behind. 'Sure. After all, we can't have you blowing our children's inheritance on bad bookkeeping.'

A crack of thunder overhead made them both jump.

Reilly fought hard to keep his face neutral, knowing that was as close to a breakthrough with Lea as he had ever got. '*Our* children?'

Furious heat flared into her face. 'Your children, of course.' The flush worsened. 'That is, your child. I don't expect…for Molly…'

He rested a calming hand on her forearm. 'Molly will always be my daughter, Lea, no matter who she lives with. If she wants Minamurra when I'm gone, she'll have it.'

Our children. The all-too-familiar kick in his guts was back, but this time it felt good, less of a kick and more of a tug. Like someone had reached low into his belly and yanked. A strangely pleasurable sensation. It wasn't sexual, although it could easily become so with very little encouragement from him. There was just something disturbingly right about sharing the office all afternoon with this woman and their child as the first big rain of the wet dumped down outside. Molly napping, Lea resting and reading, him doing the books.

It was as though they'd been doing it for ever instead of just weeks. It was now their default activity as soon as the bruising of the sky heralded rain. He'd never looked forward to a downpour so much. He'd hoped a month would be enough to get Lea—that kiss—out of his system. Spending more than a few days with a woman tended to do that, in his experience.

He'd thought it would be enough to sort his feelings about Molly out, too. But the sound of little feet pattering on timber floors was already as familiar to him as the rain splattering steadily down on Minamurra's tin roof. Loading pixie-sized bowls and cutlery into the dishwasher just felt right. Having a second breakfast with Molly after a couple of hours of early-morning outdoor work had become a pleasant ritual. The more time he spent with his daughter, the more he wanted.

Not occasionally—not once a month, not on access visits—always.

But 'always' was going to be a problem.

He stood rapidly and moved to the window, cutting Lea out of his vision and staring out to where God's Gift circled the paddock, still very much his obstinate self, even as gallons of the purest Kimberley water tumbled relentlessly onto him from the sky. It did nothing to dampen the stallion's ardour for the one female remaining in season in the next paddock.

If anything, the rain enhanced it. Every living creature out there was synchronised to the seasons and, as the air grew increasingly laden with moisture, hormones raced and every species started twitching with the sudden imperative to reproduce.

He closed his eyes and breathed in air rich with Lea's scent. Every single part of her radiated fertility. Her skin was smoother, her hair was glossier and her eyes were brighter. Her body, despite its changing shape, was fit and firm and so damned *woman* that he was cold-showering every single day.

Had he ever felt this way before? It was ridiculous to be responding to the metre of the land himself as though he'd walked its hard, red surface for thousands of years instead of just thirty-one. Knowing his child grew in Lea's fertile belly was messing with his head. The pregnant land around him was making him think things, want things, he never would have otherwise. See things that weren't there. Feel things that weren't real. Teasing him with possibilities that just wouldn't eventuate. The attractive woman, growing with the child he'd never thought he'd have. The instant family.

Lea was in this for one thing only: the stem cells that would save Molly. But it was getting complicated for her too. In the reflection of the window, he watched her hand absently stroking her rounded belly. She was bonding with their baby, whether she recognised it or not. How would she manage when the time came to hand over the child? Her heart wasn't nearly as hard as he'd always imagined, it was soft and vulnerable and liable to tear right open. The parts that weren't so obviously scarred over from a life with Bryce Curran.

He frowned. What kind of father would he be to his children? He looked at Molly again, and then let his eyes slide to the mantel above her, to the one photo in the house of the people that had raised him—a hard, emotionally distant mother and a father too tightly bound by her influence to protect his struggling son. That kind of example didn't bode well for his chances of success as a dad.

His chest tightened.

They made quite a pair—he with absolutely no idea where to begin being a good father, and Lea who'd lost her mother so young, been estranged from her father and was double-reinforced with layers of protection against any possible hurt. Both of them were hell-bound to give their child a better start in life than they had had themselves. His lips twisted on the realisation.

Just when he'd thought the only thing they had in common was Molly.

He glanced at the sky, still grey-packed but thinning out at last. He turned as he murmured Lea's name. Her eyes lifted, still guarded, but not like they had been—another change he was sure she wasn't aware of. 'Can we keep Molly up a bit later this evening? There's something I'd like you both to see.'

It was true—he did want Molly to see what he loved about Minamurra—but it was also an excuse. Just another misguided chance to spend more time with her mother.

'You'll need to bring a raincoat.'

CHAPTER TEN

'REILLY, this is crazy. I'm nearly six months' pregnant.'

Reilly peered over the roof of his feed-shed and smiled down at her. 'This from the woman who can do anything? It's just a ladder, Lea.'

One minute he wouldn't let her open a can of spaghetti without a support team, and the next he was hauling her up onto a rooftop during an electrical storm. The man was as unpredictable as the Kimberley weather. But he was impossible not to trust.

Lea caged in an excited Molly with her torso as they climbed the first few rungs of the ladder. Reilly reached down and engulfed the two little hands that stretched towards him and pulled Molly up onto the rooftop. A moment later two happy faces reappeared back over the edge.

The smaller one beaming, and as dear to Lea as her own life. The other one rapidly catching up.

She frowned and had brief words with herself; self-lectures were become a regular necessity. Reinforcing the reality of her situation was the only way she could keep herself grounded, not buying into the temporary, happy-family fantasy she was living.

'Give me your hand.' He stretched sure fingers towards her, smiling as he saw her glance nervously at the ground. 'We haul sacks of feed up these ladders, Lea. I don't think your slight weight will trouble it too much.'

Another flattering comparison, but not far off how she was feeling two thirds of the way through her pregnancy. She made a joke of it before he could. 'Not so slight these days. Better hold on tight.' She slid her clammy hand into his warm one.

'Mummy hates heights.' Molly dropped her right in it. Some reward for a lifetime of motherly service.

Reilly looked uncertain for the first time in a week. His hand closed around hers. 'Is that true, Lea?'

'I have no problem with the height,' she lied, moving cautiously up the ladder. 'It's the falling-to-certain-death part I'm less enthusiastic about.'

He chuckled and loaned her his strength as she got to the top, helping her up onto the tin roof. Molly threw small arms around her thigh.

'You did it, Mummy.'

Lea cupped her hand around her daughter's head and acknowledged Reilly's intense expression on a deep, fortifying breath. 'What?'

He shook his head, his eyes growing cryptic. 'I didn't think you were afraid of anything.'

'Respecting the true nature of something is not the same as being afraid of it. Unenclosed heights, by their nature, are dangerous.' She glanced to ensure Molly was well back from the edge.

'You'll find danger anywhere if you go looking for it. The trick is to be open to all the possibilities, not just the negative ones.'

Maybe in the world you come from. 'Such as?'

He steered them to the centre of the roof where three deck-chairs and an esky were set up facing west. Molly hopped straight into the smallest of the three chairs. Reilly took Lea's shoulders and turned her to the coastal horizon. 'Such as the amazing view an unenclosed high place might afford you when it's not trying to kill you.'

Lea's breath caught and she sank down onto one of the chairs. From the rooftop, they had a completely unobscured view across Minamurra to the coastal ranges, where the gods of electricity and earth battled it out in spectacular fashion.

The sky was a deep, dark orange as the last fingers of the setting sun reached across it. Brilliant forks of light split the horizon, streaking bright patterns down towards earth. Strike after strike compounded into a blazing, criss-crossing light-show that eclipsed anything humans could create.

Lea sighed and stroked Molly's hair as she squealed and laughed, knowing they were making yet another unforgettable memory. She was pleased that Reilly featured in so many of them.

Molly would need those when they parted. *So will you,* a tiny voice whispered.

As the sun disappeared finally to the west, the lightning was all that lit the sky; a thousand little forks caused the thick, gathering clouds to glow into a luminous, cumulative mass. Deadly, but beautiful. She turned slightly towards Reilly and her eyes widened to find him already looking at her, lightning bolts reflected in their dark depths.

A hint of heat crept up her throat. 'Is this wise?'

Static charge filled his eyes. They flicked to her lips. 'Probably not. But it feels good, doesn't it?'

The heat doubled. 'I meant sitting on a tin roof during an electrical storm. It can't be safe.'

His eyes skipped away briefly and when they returned they were more guarded. 'The storm is over the coast. Miles away.' He paused. 'You really expect the worst from life, don't you?'

Lea chose her words carefully, aware of the little ears so close by. 'I've seen what life can do.'

Reilly considered that in silence. 'How many beautiful experiences will it take to outweigh all the negative ones you hold onto?'

Lea bristled. 'I don't hold onto them. They just *are.*'

He shook his head. 'You're missing so much.'

She straightened in her seat. 'I find my own beauty. My own way.' *In my own time.*

His eyes were unrelenting. 'I'm glad. Everyone deserves some happiness.'

Lea wrapped her arms around her body despite the cloying heat of the night. 'We aren't talking about happiness, we're talking about life. I'm happy.'

'You think so?'

She burned to answer him more directly, but was critically

conscious of Molly sitting so close by. She kept her voice light, calm. 'Everyone experiences happiness differently, Reilly.'

He conceded that. 'What makes you happy? I'd like to know.'

She slid her eyes sideways to her daughter.

His narrowed. 'There must be more. What brought you joy before?'

Before Molly, after Molly. She remembered accusing Anna of measuring her life the same way with Jared, remembered trying to tell her how unhealthy that was. Yet here she was doing the same thing. Except she was putting that load on a five-year-old child.

She turned her face back to the sky-show on a frown and didn't answer. The storm was too far away to bring much more than a distant rumble, but the night was thick with the amphibian chorus, hundreds of barking, croaking, whooping frogs.

Reilly sighed and then spoke over the cacophony. 'We're sitting up here in front of the most beautiful show in nature and we're arguing. How can that be?'

Because you're judging me. And finding me wanting. Her instincts told her to stay silent, to let it go, avoid it. But something else egged her on. She turned back to him.

'I've spent my life disappointing people, Reilly. Trying to live up to expectations I didn't have a chance of meeting. Yet here I am finding out—once again—that my definition of happiness, the way I find it and demonstrate it, isn't enough for you.' She turned back to the horizon, keeping her voice casual for Molly's sake. The effort exhausted her. 'You're measuring me by your own standards instead of letting me just live my own.'

The lightning show went on. Finally, Reilly spoke again. 'What do you want, Lea?'

She stared at him, deeply saddened, and whispered furiously under the rumbly thunder so only he could hear. 'I want a miracle. I want a miracle that means that Molly gets to live and I don't have to give up my child. I don't want to see this baby once a month and then hand it back to you. Some days I think I'd rather not see it at all once it's born. And then I wonder what would happen if I didn't hand it over—if I just ran off into this enormous country with both my children and disappeared.'

Her voice broke. 'But I don't want you to be alone either. You're a good man, Reilly Martin, and you deserve your miracle too. I can't take that from you.' Anguish thickened her voice, and compounding lightning-flashes turned his face into a living modernist painting. 'I want a solution where everybody wins. And I know that's never going to happen. That's not how life works.'

The intensity in his stare rivalled the natural show playing out on the horizon. 'What if miracles don't happen?'

'Then one of us is going to be in agony in three months' time. I really don't want it to be me.' She dropped her head, flushing, then continued, whispering. 'And I really don't want it to be you. What should I do, Reilly? Tell me what to do.'

He shook his head mutely.

'And you have to ask why I don't expect the best from life?' She stood and gave a yawning Molly a gentle nudge. It killed her to have to wait for Reilly's help over by the ladder, but she wasn't about to risk the baby—Molly's future—just to make a point. She stood quietly at the roof's edge. Reilly took Molly's hand in his and then gave Lea his other hand to steady her onto the ladder.

For the briefest of lightning flashes the three of them were connected as a family and Lea's heart squeezed. She took a firm hold of the ladder with both hands, breaking the connection.

What they had was so transient, the comfortable togetherness born out of necessity and convenience as the wet season got into full swing. The idea of them being a family was a pretty, fleeting show, just like the lightning.

It was an insubstantial illusion.

'Merry Christmas, Mummy.' Molly's serious face where she stood, tiny, by Lea's bed was level with her own. Despite her exhaustion, Lea let her lips spread in a welcoming smile for her daughter.

'Merry Christmas, baby.' She struggled up onto her elbows, noticing the tiniest hint of light outside. 'What time is it?'

Little brown eyes lit by the bedside lamp widened. 'I don't know.'

Lea chuckled and reached for her watch. She laughed outright then. 'Molly, it's four-thirty in the morning.' Then she noticed her daughter's face, paler even than her usual anaemic porcelain. She sat up, wide awake. 'What's wrong?'

Serious, round eyes were yet to blink. 'What if Santa can't find us?'

She wasn't sick. The adrenaline-burst played out in Lea's system, trembling her hands. Santa-related crises she could deal with.

'Tell you what,' she said, swinging her legs over the edge of the bed. 'Let's go check out the living room, see if he's left anything under your tree.'

Reilly had insisted on a proper tree—a strapling eucalypt in a giant pot—and on decorating it from boxes full of designer decorations he'd had flown in. It hadn't occurred to Lea to pack any of their Christmas things, and Molly had been unexpectedly upset at not having her little wooden soldiers to hang. In the end, Reilly had put away most of the expensive baubles and tinsel in favour of some older ones that Agnes Dawes had ferreted out of a back shed.

Molly had fallen on the family hand-me-downs like they were Kimberley diamonds. In a crazy way, they were worth more. The resulting tree was bottom heavy, the bulk of the wooden decorations applied too far to the left and at five-year-old height, but it was the first tree Molly had ever decorated herself and that made it perfect.

She skipped over now to look under it. Even in the early-morning light, Lea could see there wasn't much there. A simple gift from Lea herself—a practical selection of new clothes—and one or two other festive-looking boxes. No toy-store selection. She breathed a sigh of relief.

He'd remembered.

Molly picked up an oversized envelope from the tree and ran towards Lea. She could see from the letter that it was addressed to *Miss Molly Curran* in big, cartoon letters. She bent down to take it from her daughter, but she ran straight past.

'What's this, Reilly?'

Lea stiffened, suddenly conscious that she was in her pyjamas, ungroomed and sleep-deprived. The baby had kept her up late. Her hand got halfway to her hair before she steeled herself to smile him a good-morning. Her belly flip-flopped; disgusting how good he could look before dawn. Then again, he was probably used to getting up at this time.

'I don't know, but it's addressed to you,' he said. 'Shall I open it?'

Molly squealed, jumped up and down and then doubled over in a hacking cough. It took her a moment to recover but, when she did, she just wiped her mouth carefully and then gave Reilly a huge grin.

Lea saw the despair flit across his eyes and then he, too, put on a brave face.

'It's from Santa,' Reilly read out with exaggerated care. Lea smiled at their daughter's barely contained excitement. '"Dear Molly. I was surprised to find you not at Yurraji but, fortunately, a passing bandicoot told me where you were and I was able to follow his directions to Minamurra".'

Molly's enormous eyes were never going to recover from the excitement of this Christmas morning.

'"I could barely fit your gift through the door,"' he read on, '"So I've left it outside for you. I hope you don't mind".'

He read Santa's sign-off as Molly sprinted for the door. He and Lea both called at the same time, 'Walk!'

Reilly's grin was as big as the house as he followed her outside, as though this was his first Christmas instead of his thirty-first. Molly's search-light gaze darted around, looking for clues. Reilly's eyes went to the stables.

Lea froze. *No...*

'Why don't we try over there?' he suggested casually and set off in a straight line to the stables.

He'd got Molly her own horse! Anger bubbled up deep inside Lea. Hadn't they been through the whole 'big gift' thing back in October? Her lips were tight as she caught up with him striding towards the building. 'Reilly...'

He ignored her hissed whisper and led Molly into the dark

of the stables. A switch-flip later the building glowed into bright light. A stone formed where her heart should be. She turned to berate him just as Molly let off the kind of eardrum-splitting squeal only a five-year-old could produce. Every horse in the place shied in its stall. Lea followed her eyes to the back corner of the stables to a cubby-house made of straw bales. It had a big, hand-painted sign above the door that said: MOLLY'S PLACE.

It was simple, thoughtful, safe…and utterly, utterly perfect.

Lea watched through tear-washed eyes as Molly scampered through the front door to explore the tiny interior. Her chest ached.

'You told me about all the hours you spent hiding out in the hay store when you were younger. I thought it would be good for Molly to have her own space when she visits. Somewhere she can play without wearing her out.'

He'd managed to find the perfect gift for Molly and give Lea one too: a future. The illusion that everything really was going to be okay. She swallowed the tears and just nodded. In the corner of her vision, she saw Reilly glance down at his boots, and then she heard him clear his throat too.

They watched Molly play in silence. Poor old Max the cat chose that moment to wander in to check out all the early-morning commotion, and Molly immediately scooped him up and disappeared into the straw cubby-house with her reluctant best friend.

Lea had recovered her composure by then. 'Thank you, Reilly,' she said simply, her voice thick. 'It's a wonderful Christmas gift.'

Every day that passed she found it harder to ignore his goodness, the thoughtful things he did. The way he watched out for Molly. For her. It was completely at odds with the man who had handed her that contract. It made it harder to keep the line safely drawn in the sand.

Max exploded out of the cubby-house with Molly in hot pursuit and Reilly swooped in to rescue him, scooping a wheezing Molly up into his arms. She settled there happily then flung her arms around his neck and pressed her mouth hard against his face.

Reilly's eyes fell shut and he brought his other hand up to press his daughter harder to him. Lea's throat constricted. It was the first kiss Molly had ever given him.

A charged moment passed before she whispered to Reilly, eyeing Lea the whole time.

Oh, that little minx...

'Yes it is, Molly.' Reilly spoke with exaggerated loudness. 'It's a perfect time to give Mummy her Christmas gift.'

Molly bounced in Reilly's strong hold but he didn't put her down. He leaned forward and placed his hand on Lea's shoulder, then gently turned her to the back stalls. Two long, familiar faces stared back at her from adjoining stalls, wondering what all the fuss was about.

'Goff. Pan.' Lea rushed to their stall, pressing her face between them and running her hand up their necks to tangle in their manes. They stood obligingly for her affectionate assault. The tears threatened again. 'When did...?'

'Yesterday,' he said simply while Molly beamed in his arms. 'While you were resting. We snuck them in.'

Oh, I've missed you. Lea didn't know how much until she felt another tiny piece of her heart heal over. She breathed in their familiar, horsey scent.

Her throat tightened dangerously and she called on her birth breathing to keep the tears at bay. Confusion washed over her. Why did he keep doing such kind things? Wasn't this going above and beyond the terms of their arrangement, Christmas or no Christmas? It really wasn't helping her patrol her emotional fence-line.

'Lea? Are you okay?'

The gentle query in his voice as he lowered Molly back to the ground was her undoing. She turned away from his eyes, from her horses, from her child, and walked straight out of the stables. Tears almost blinded her but she forced her feet to keep moving.

'Hey, Lea.' He jogged after her.

'You can't do this, Reilly. It's not fair.' The words were almost a sob, back over her shoulder.

'Do what?'

Her chest squeezed hard. 'This.' She waved her arms at the stables, at the house, at herself. 'Doing lovely things. Being so kind. You need to stop.'

Complete confusion bathed his face. 'I don't understand.'

'It doesn't help me.' She turned and nearly shouted at him, pressing a hand to her belly as though it would protect the child within from the tumult of emotion. 'You're making it too hard.'

She turned and struck out for the house again, miserable and horrified at how much she'd already said. What it implied. He caught up with her and circled her shoulder, pulling her to a sudden halt. His eyes appealed. 'Explain it to me, Lea. What am I doing?'

She spun around, the thick mud of her tears choking her. 'I'm bonding, damn it!'

He reeled back from her anger. 'With the baby?'

'With the baby. With you.' Disgust dripped from every word. 'I can't bond with you, Reilly.'

He froze and stared. When he spoke it was quiet. Simplistic. 'Why not?'

'Why not?' Her voice squeaked the question. 'We have three months to get through, and then you walk away with my baby. It's going to be hard enough to—'

Her mouth snapped shut. *Idiot.* She'd said too much. She'd just handed him the perfect tool to hurt her. The sounds of the morning dropped completely away, leaving only the thrumming of Lea's blood past her ears. She fought desperately not to close her eyes against the inevitable.

'Then don't.'

The breath punched out of her. 'What?'

'Don't hand the baby over. Don't walk away. Stay.'

She stared at him, horrified.

'We can be a family. You, me and Molly. And the new baby.' He made it sound so insanely simple. 'Stay, Lea.'

'You want us to stay? How long?'

'For ever. Molly's grandchildren could grow up here.'

For ever. The parts of her that were tired of being lonely responded unanimously to that idea. *Yes, yes, yes.*

'We're compatible.' Reilly brushed her hot cheek to make his point. Her skin leapt at the caress. 'We get along well enough. We both love Molly. We could make it work.' He reached up and smoothed her hair from her damp face, his eyes appealing. 'Molly could have a proper brother or sister and the baby could have a full-time mother.'

She stared, wide-eyed, trying not to savour the feel of his fingers on her face.

'Be open to all the possibilities, Lea. Just think about it.'

Her voice was no more than a whisper. 'You want a family that much?'

'As much as you did nearly six years ago.'

She slipped her hand to her belly to protect the innocent life within. Her child. The planet's gravity seemed to shift and caused a delirious weightlessness in her. If she said yes, she wouldn't have to give up her baby after all. It was the perfect solution.

And the absolute worst.

'What about love?' she whispered.

He paled. 'A lot of relationships start without love. And last a lifetime.'

Her gut twisted. She'd already done that for the first half of her life, she wasn't about to do it for the rest. And she wasn't about to expose her daughter to that either.

'It's for the children,' he urged, as though that would somehow make it better.

Unshed tears clogged her throat. She was the price Reilly was prepared to pay to have a family. A necessary evil. He might not completely loathe her any more—late-night kisses had a way of sorting that—but he very clearly did not love her. How could he and still want to take her child? She had a contract with his signature on it that spelled their arrangement out very clearly, regardless of what fanciful thoughts she had in the tiny hours of the night.

This was about Molly. This was about the unborn child she carried.

This was about Martin heirs.

And she had committed to doing whatever it took to save

her child. Lately that sentiment had broadened out to include her unborn one as well. Time was running out and the miracle she was hoping for just hadn't eventuated.

She swiped at the tears on her face. 'Is this a new condition of the contract?'

'Lea, no.' Brown eyes blazed. 'It's not a condition. It's a...'

Don't say 'proposal,' please... She might just break.

'It's an offer. An offer you are free to decline. But think about the children.'

As he so clearly was.

All of this was about the children.

CHAPTER ELEVEN

HE WAS willing to play dirty if he had to.

Reilly cursed inwardly as he ground the gears of his beloved Land Rover, moving back up to speed after slowing for a couple of stray cattle on the road to the homestead. Molly happily peered out the window next to him.

This morning's piece of brilliance had been spontaneous, opportunistic, but he'd had time to plan since then. Almost half of Christmas day. He hadn't handled it well; Lea's underwhelmed reaction told him that. He had no experience at asking a woman to spend her life with him. It really wasn't the sort of thing you could train for.

She'd been predictably pessimistic, immediately naming the biggest hurdle to their success: the absence of love between them.

Having it pointed out so practically was a kick in the ribs, but he hadn't expected anything less. She was with him for legal and practical reasons. For his genes. Lasting romances just didn't start that way.

They didn't start with two lots of blackmail, either.

But a friendship could, and friendship could take them right through until their grey years. He'd seen it happen out here. It wasn't perfect, but it was something. She wasn't entirely immune to him, either. Her body responded to his now every bit as much as it had back then. It could be enough. There were much worse things than being friends with a beautiful, intelligent woman, the mother of your children.

Like being alone.

It was not why he did it but, sitting on the roof of his feed-shed, he'd suddenly seen the foolishness of the contract he'd asked her to sign. The inevitable impossibility of a woman like Lea being able to give up her baby. She didn't want a conventional relationship—she'd said so—so why not an unconventional and extremely practical one?

Surely that would have to resonate with the queen of unconventionality?

But just in case it didn't, his campaign of persuasion would start today.

'Mum!' Molly sat up straighter in the passenger seat and looked towards the house as he pulled up in front of the house. Lea burst out of the front door and hurried down the steps towards them. Molly hopped happily out of the passenger side and met her mother halfway. Lea swung her up into her arms, pressed her close then turned for the house.

'Where have you been, Molly? I was so worried.'

Reilly took a deep breath. 'You were napping so soundly and Molly wasn't tired. We went for a drive.' He scooted up the steps behind her.

Lea pushed back into the house, her body stiff. 'Without telling me?'

'We left you a note.'

She spun around. 'What? Where?'

He led her into the kitchen and leaned casually on the stainless-steel fridge, keeping his hands hidden. His note was stuck with a magnet in the middle of the door.

Colour flamed up her face. 'Who leaves a note on the fridge door?'

He laughed. 'Everyone, Lea. You've been alone too long.'

She blushed further. 'I thought… Never mind. I'm just glad you're back.'

Molly squirmed to be out of her mother's death-grip. 'Happy Christmas, Mum.'

She looked at her daughter patiently, putting her down. 'We've done Christmas, Molly.'

Reilly slowly brought his hands around. 'Uh, not quite. Molly wanted to get you a present. She asked me to take her.'

Molly beamed as he handed Lea the fistful of wildflowers they'd selected. 'Molly had very specific flowers in mind and it took us a bit longer to find just the right ones.'

As her eyes fell on the chaotic cluster of freshly picked wildflowers, they completely changed. Bled pale. His stomach clenched.

'Native iris,' she whispered.

'Yes, amongst others. Do you like them?'

She nodded and swallowed hard. 'They're my favourite.'

'They were my grandma's favourite,' Molly proudly added from the floor.

Lea looked at her hard. 'How do you know that?'

Molly looked uncertain suddenly in the face of her mother's intensity. Reilly dropped to his haunches in a show of silent support.

She edged closer to him, her voice small. 'You told Aunt Sapphie that day.'

Lea must have seen her daughter's growing discomfort; she slid a hand out onto her shoulder and gentled her speech. 'What day, honey?'

Big brown eyes nearly broke Reilly's heart as Molly added, 'The day you cried.'

The only sound in the kitchen was the clock ticking. Reilly desperately wanted to wrap his arms around Lea. She looked like she was about to shatter. Her lashes blinked furiously.

Instead, he did the only thing he could. 'What a great Christmas this has been, huh?' He pulled Molly close to his side. 'A great cubby-house, beautiful flowers. And I got to spend some time with my special girl.'

Molly looked bereft. 'I didn't get you a present.'

Reilly chuckled, falling even harder for his wonderful little girl with a heart as big as the Dawson Ranges. 'You know what gift I'd really like?' Molly shook her head. 'A kiss. Right here.' He pointed at his cheek.

Molly hit him with a double-dimple, super-shy smile and

rolled her eyes. Reilly wondered at what age 'boy germs' kicked in. Then she flung her arms around his neck and gave him a huge smacker right on the spot he'd identified. It eclipsed the one in the stables tenfold.

Lea crossed to the pantry to get a vase to display the wild-flowers, visibly struggling to pull herself together.

'What did you get Reilly, Mum?'

Hazel eyes flew up to his.

He should help her out. Really, it would be the right thing to do. Instead, he leaned back on the fridge and smiled.

Molly reminded her theatrically. 'He got you Pan and Goff.'

Mental note to self: put Molly on the payroll. She was un-questionably worth as much as any man on his team. He smiled. 'She's got a point, Lea.'

Lea glared at him. 'I guess I'll have to give that some thought later, huh?'

'Christmas is nearly over. You should give him a kiss too. Right here.' Molly touched the place on her face that Reilly had touched on his. She was deadly serious.

Oh, her wages had just doubled.

Lea's lips thinned. 'Maybe I could think of something else.'

'I'd be happy to have whatever you gave Molly last year.' His eyes locked on hers. He remembered their conversation seven months ago.

I gave her me. I was hers to do whatever she wanted to...all day.

Lea glared at him, unmoved. 'I'll take the kiss, thanks.'

'That would be a great Christmas present,' he said for Molly's sake, and then for Lea's. 'A kiss from *two* beautiful women.' Her eyes flamed magnificently. She took her time ar-ranging the wildflowers, rinsing her hands and finally drying them. Molly watched patiently. Reilly was ready to snap.

She turned back, walked up to him rigid-backed, and lifted her eyes to his. 'Merry Christmas, Reilly,' she whispered politely right before she stretched up onto her toes and pressed her lips to his cheek where Molly had.

He couldn't help it; he just wasn't that strong a man. He

turned his cheek just slightly—a breath—but enough that her soft mouth landed on the corner of his. She jerked back on a gasp but his hand at her back kept her close. He looked down into enormous, hazel irises framing flared pupils. He drowned in them. Every part of him was aware of her. The fertile hardness of her belly. Her scent. Her body heat. The softness of her hair.

Not touching her was going to be a challenge.

If she agreed to stay.

Her hands rested softly on his hammering chest and pushed slowly away. It reminded him of their killer kiss in this very kitchen. He let her go and her eyes lifted back to his. Awareness filled them.

Time stopped.

His mouth dried.

A huge challenge.

'Max!'

The cat streaked off as soon as it heard Molly's delighted shriek. Mother and father both snapped their faces in the direction she'd taken off.

'Molly, walk!'

It only took a week of solid rain before the parched land was bloated and drunk; the rich Kimberley red earth couldn't soak up another drop. Billabongs grew, rivers burst their banks, new ones formed in unlikely places and roads flooded. Minamurra was packed to its rafters with everything they needed to see them through the isolation of the wet season.

Lea scooted down more comfortably on the outdoor seating on the veranda and sipped her tea as the rain drummed down. She loved this time of year because everyone went into lockdown, and keeping to yourself, your property, became the norm. No one judged you for it when everyone did it. It was the perfect time to be alone.

Except this year she wasn't.

She was on a station with a dozen people. And Reilly.

Who was still waiting for her answer. Who'd been nothing

but patient since throwing her world into upheaval last week with his awkward proposition. She couldn't think of it as a proposal, he hadn't technically asked her to marry him, although she figured that was what would happen if she stayed. Or maybe not. Maybe they could pull off the kind of relationship Agnes Dawes had with her Frank—being together but living apart. Except in their case it would be living together, being apart.

How sad.

The baby sympathised, sending her the reassuring feather of its touch. Lea smiled. She was getting positively fanciful in the late stages of her pregnancy.

She let her thoughts go back to her handsome host. It was amazing that he hadn't demanded an answer before now. He would have been within his rights given their situation. Instead, he just watched her when he thought she wasn't looking, assessing, contemplating. Brooding. It seemed they were always together, and not just because of the wet. A thousand little things kept bringing them back into each other's presence. Every one seemed legitimate on the surface, but Lea tried to think back to pre-Christmas. Had they had this level of interaction then? Or was she just noticing it now? Now that she was so sensitised to it.

'Lea?'

Her head drifted towards his voice like a lily on a pond tide. 'Good morning.'

He slid his akubra off his head as he approached along the wide veranda. His hair was as damp as his skin from working outdoors. Or maybe fresh from the shower, it was impossible to tell. Certainly it was humid enough already this morning to be either.

'All set for a new year?'

God, was it New Year? She really was out of touch. 'I wondered what all the activity was down at the barn.' The barn was where the ringers all shared accommodation.

He perched his length on the veranda balustrade. 'They're having a party tonight. To see in the New Year. You're invited, if you'd like to come.'

Lea's heart raced. She never celebrated New Year, she never

seemed to have much to look forward to each year. Sharing it with a group of strangers…

Her indecision must have shown on her face.

'If you'd rather not, then we can stay home. I'll need to make a brief appearance, but then I can come back up here, spend it with you and Molly.'

Like a family. Her chest squeezed. But Molly would be in bed by seven, and then they would be alone. On New Year's Eve. With the whole 'midnight' thing ticking closer. She thought about that kiss in the kitchen.

Her heart pumped harder. 'No. I'd like to go. They've been really good with Molly and me. Very kind and understanding.'

And there was safety in numbers.

'Great. We'll head down as soon as Molly's asleep. They're slow-cooking a sheep all afternoon.'

His wry smile had her wondering if she'd just been played. Maybe she had; she'd just agreed to her first public outing with him. She nodded. Reilly's eyes darted around the veranda. 'Was there something else?' she said.

His chest expanded on a slow breath. 'There's a rodeo on Valentine's Day. I'm signed on to run pick-up.' He watched her carefully. 'I wondered if you would go with me. Mrs Dawes could watch Molly.'

It was very telling that the thought of being out with him in public bothered her a lot more than the thought of going to a rodeo. 'A Valentine's Day rodeo.' She'd worked hard to perfect her one-eyebrow lift. 'How romantic.'

'Welcome to the north,' he smiled, then turned serious. 'I want people to understand that you and Molly are now under my protection. That they mess with me if they don't treat you respectfully.'

'And me sitting in the bleachers at a rodeo, over seven months pregnant, will do that how, exactly? The gossips will have a field day.'

He squatted next to her and ran his knuckles gently over her swollen belly. 'Are you ashamed of what we've done? Of being pregnant?'

She stared at him, surprised. How odd that she wasn't. She felt none of the shame about the way she'd brought Molly into existence. Her voice was breathy. 'No.'

'Then let them talk. This way it gets it out in public. No more hiding, Lea.'

There was only one reason that would be important. Her mouth dried. 'You're assuming I'm staying for good.'

His gaze was enigmatic. 'I'm counting on it. It's the only choice you can make.'

Reilly was building castles for himself and their children. He was forcing her hand. The grey skies seemed to close in that little bit more. Her pulse picked up and she changed the subject. 'What are we doing until seven?'

He straightened and crossed to the coat rack that stood by the door, then heaved his heavy oilskin-coat on. How he didn't swelter in all that gear in the heat of the wet season...

His eyes dulled over carefully. 'I don't know about you, but I'm training all day with Cooper. He thinks the Yurraji mares might both be pregnant, so we need to get them gentled as soon as possible.'

It was crazy to be disappointed at the thought of a whole day without Reilly. Not when he was offering her a lifetime with him. Seven o'clock suddenly seemed a long way off. Still, there was no shortage of things to do. Molly was due to start distance ed this year and she had a pile of assessment tests to take so that the city-based service could design a programme for her first year of schooling. And Lea's brokers were waiting to hear back from her on some acquisitions.

She'd finally accepted Reilly's contribution to the ICSI treatment and Molly's medical costs and had paid her portfolio back the money she'd siphoned off. If she was considering a lifetime with Reilly she didn't want to come to him with nothing of her own. Her pride just wouldn't allow it.

Not that she was doing more than considering it, her subconscious rushed to remind her.

'Okay, I guess I'll see you around seven, then.'

Reilly turned for the paddocks and tugged his hat down

firmly. 'It's a dress-up thing, Lea. The one night of the year…'
He dipped his head and stepped out into the pummelling rain.

What sort of 'dress-up' would Reilly choose? A tux was definitely out, but what about a suit? A fancy land-baron ensemble? She'd never seen him in anything other than casual station-wear. Her cheeks flamed as she remembered that wasn't true. She'd seen quite a lot of him in nothing at all. She fanned her cheeks as if that would temper the spreading blush. Forbidden images clamoured for prominence. She battled them all back and looked over to the feed-shed.

She'd sat atop its roof only a week or so ago and begged Reilly for an answer. A miracle. He'd handed her one that ensured neither of them had to endure the agony of the loss of a child. Surely this decision should be a no-brainer?

Why then was it hurting her so much to make it?

'You look…'
Reilly stood framed by the kitchen doorway, his eyes carefully neutral.

Lea had a panic moment, thinking she'd chosen inappropriately. And at how excited she was to see him again; it had only been a few hours. She ran nervous hands down her wraparound dress over her bulging belly and disguised her discomfort in humour. 'Heavily pregnant?'

'Beautifully pregnant,' he corrected. He stepped out of the shadows towards her. 'Where have you been keeping that dress?'

The chocolate wraparound was her primary pregnancy-outfit. Because it criss-crossed her ever-expanding breasts and belly and tied at her hip, she could wear it when she was small or in the last weeks of her pregnancy. It was about the only thing she'd brought with her that was suitable for a party. Reilly's smoky eyes reminded her how closely the light fabric followed the contours of her body.

We're compatible, he'd said. Right now she was feeling a heck of a lot more than compatible. Sexual awareness swirled around her legs with the brown fabric.

She shuffled nervously, ignoring it. 'It's not formal, I know.'

'It's perfect.' He leaned on the corner of the kitchen table. His moss-green shearer's top stretched across broad worker's shoulders, and distressed leather boots peeked out from beneath spotless moleskin trousers. Country formal—but of course!

'Molly's asleep?'

'Even playing in her straw fort wears her out these days. She went down early.'

Reilly frowned. 'Are you worried about her?'

Every day. But she didn't want Reilly worrying. 'No. She's fine. It's to be expected.' She stroked her belly and Reilly's eyes followed every move. 'A few months more and she'll start feeling very different.'

'Right. The stem cells.' His brown eyes darkened and he pushed himself to his feet. 'Shall we?'

They strolled the long distance between Minamurra's homestead and the ringers' quarters. By cosmic cooperation, the rain had let up for the party, but the air was still drenched with humidity and Lea was sticky by the time they reached the barn. She sighed as the cooler indoor air kissed her damp skin. Her only consolation was that everyone else was in the same predicament. Coat jackets littered the barn and the party-goers were already well into the evening's festivities.

The first hour was a drain for Lea. She and Reilly took it in turns to tiptoe back to the homestead to check on a sleeping Molly, and in those minutes that he was gone she felt the familiar panic of someone who wasn't good socially. Agnes Dawes rescued her the first time and sought her help with tossing salads for the feast to come.

But as the second hour wore on she realised she wasn't hating it. Reilly's team were respectful for the most part, certainly towards her in her pregnant state—even though many of them were young and clearly excited by the rare presence of both alcohol and a handful of eligible women at the same time. Agnes tried to fill her in as best she could, but Lea lost track of the complicated connections between them all. Ultimately, it didn't matter. They were Reilly's team or friends of Reilly's team.

It suddenly dawned on her that some of the men were also

friends of Reilly. And, judging by the speculation she saw in a few hastily disguised glances, some of the women. Suddenly the party, and the possibility of spending a lifetime with Reilly, took on a whole new meaning. Would he expect her to become friends with these people too? Would she want to? Buying into Reilly's life on Minamurra was one thing. The real world was a whole different kettle of fish.

When it was just the two of them, stranded on the station in the wet, it wasn't impossible to imagine herself growing old here with Reilly. Watching their two children growing up into healthy, happy adults.

It was almost possible to imagine herself happy—not deliriously, but at least content.

Giving up a child should have been the hardest decision she'd ever made. It was ridiculous still to be deciding whether or not to stay. Was spending a lifetime with a complex, charismatic man that big a price for the gift of two children? A man who had more than enough capacity to love both children. Who, she knew in her heart, would be faithful to the commitment he made her as his children's mother.

Who would honour her even if he couldn't love her.

The party buzzed on around them and Lea caught herself enjoying several conversations with locals. She endured a few cold-shoulders too—the endorsement of the king of the circuit hadn't worked a complete miracle with the small district population—but for the most part it got easier to mix with the others as the night wore on. Maybe it had something to do with the prodigious amount of alcohol that was consumed as the hours ticked by. Beer-goggles seemed to make her more acceptable to all of them.

The slow-cooked lamb was succulent and delicious, even after being sliced into too-thick slices, shoved inelegantly into fresh, tasty buns and drowned in native-mint jelly. Full bellies seemed to slow the alcohol consumption and the group split into two: those who were still drinking and those who had stopped for the evening. Or never started, in Lea's case.

'Would you like to dance, Lea?'

Reilly's hot breath on her naked neck sent shivers right through her as he came up behind her. He reached round her to hand her a glass of iced water. She took a healthy swallow.
'I… No, thank you. I don't dance.'

'Don't or can't? There are no heights involved.'

If you didn't count the great fall her heart was likely to take if she let him touch her. 'I don't feel particularly graceful at the moment.' *Coward. Hiding behind the baby.*

'What if I promised to help you?' His eyes blazed in the low light. They were like lips along her collarbone.

One dance. How bad could that be? It wasn't as if anything inappropriate could happen in a room full of people. Her skin tingled, dying to be touched. Knowing she really shouldn't. It wouldn't be smart. It was hard enough seeing him every day.

Reilly slipped his hand into hers, large and sure, and led her, unresisting, the few metres to where tables had been pushed back, creating an informal dance-floor for those enjoying the slower music. He turned his body into hers and slipped one hand around to rest on her waist, warm and large. The fingers threaded firmly through hers curled intimately close to their bodies. Air caught in her throat.

Breathe…

Her chocolate-coloured dress threatened to melt into a gooey, brown mess everywhere her body touched Reilly's—her protruding belly, primarily, which seemed to heat up like a stone in the desert. Her hips, occasionally her thighs. And the whole time the seductive warmth of the strong arms encircling her burned through her like a brand. As if the evening wasn't steamy enough already.

It's only chemistry…

'You feel amazing.' Reilly flushed the moment the murmured words left his lips, as though he hadn't meant to speak them aloud.

Breathe… She kept her eyes on the top button of his shirt, where his collarbone dipped in an intriguing hollow she remembered once pressing her lips to. The harder she fought not to think about this thing zinging between them, the more her body chose to remember. She struggled to keep it light. 'You just like the inflatable boobs.'

He chuckled. 'I'd be lying if I said I didn't. But it's more than that. Every part of you is so alive, so healthy.' His voice dropped low. 'It's very...compelling.'

Lea fortified urgently. 'You won't be saying that when you have to tie my shoes for me.'

'You don't believe me?' His gaze was intense as they swayed on the spot. 'I'd be happy to prove it to you.'

Surely he could feel her wildly hammering heart? They were standing that close he could probably feel the baby's. 'I'm sure you would.'

He stepped around her attempt to brush him off.

'This is what I see when I look at you.' He leaned in closer, to murmur into her ear. Every other sound faded into the background—the music, the laughter, the buzz of conversation going on around them. 'Your eyes first. So bright and clear. Their depths, when you let me in.'

She rolled the eyes he was admiring, already horribly uncomfortable with his scrutiny. He lifted their joined hands to touch her mouth with his thumb, undeterred. 'Then your lips, remembering how they felt against mine. How they shape when you smile. How they tremble when you cry.'

His eyes held hers captive. It hurt to breathe. She certainly didn't have enough air to make even a weak joke. His hand trailed down her throat, across the creamy expanse of her *décolletage*, then twisted carefully so that her own folded fingers brushed the swell of her breast, curved around under it. They trembled. His eyes dipped to her cleavage briefly then lifted back to her eyes. She throbbed where he'd looked.

'Your beautiful breasts... Life-giving. Spectacular. Some days when I'm tired I just want to lay my head there and sleep for ever.'

Lea's breath caught on a half-sob. What cruel irony was this? She'd waited a lifetime for someone to worship her this way. Why, when it finally came, was it with someone who wanted her physically but didn't want *her*?

'And this...' Reilly's fingers opened around hers and splayed across the top of her pregnant stomach and pressed between them privately like they belonged there. His lips brushed against her ear, hypnotically. She trembled in his arms. 'The flesh that sustains my child, that nurtures my future. The sexiest part of all. This child connects us, Lea. As it grows, so does the link between us. You must feel that?'

How could only words be so devastating? She broke away on a cry, stumbled free of the dance floor and made for the door.

He wanted a family, not her.

'Lea?' He was right behind her.

She put her hand up to stall him, desperate to be away from his seductive presence. 'I have to check on Molly.' Then her shaky legs took her out of the door into the darkness.

Reilly let her go, kicking himself for letting his guard down. It was too much; she wasn't ready to hear how much he wanted her. But he did. He burned with it. He'd started out wanting to show her how they could be together. That they still had the same chemistry from years before. That they could still find a connection. But then he'd taken her in his arms...

He'd never let himself lose it like that in a public place, not with someone he respected. Cared for. He frowned.

Cared for? When had sexual attraction become *caring*? His eyes looked after her, an unfamiliar surge of heat flowing out from his midsection. Lea wasn't a woman he could afford to care for. She was only in this for Molly's sake, ultimately. If she stayed with him at all it would be to avoid losing the new baby. To keep her family together. She was too high-risk an investment to stake anything more than hope on.

Yet he could feel himself giving more.

The crowded room choked him suddenly. He turned for th house and sprinted after Lea. He caught up with her near the grassy hill that led up to the homestead. The sound of the party continued from the far paddock in the quiet of the night.

'Lea, I'm sorry.' He forced himself not to touch her, not trusting himself.

She stumbled to a halt, turned. 'I can't do it, Reilly.' Her voice was tragic.

His knotted stomach unravelled and threatened to spill out onto the dirt. 'Do what?'

'This. Us.' She waved panicked hands. He burned to take one in his and reassure her. She lifted miserable eyes to his. 'If I'm to stay, we can't... There can't...'

If I'm to stay. 'You're not attracted to me?' Even he knew that would be a lie. But it still hurt to think it.

She sighed. 'Attraction was never our problem.'

A primitive part of him roared. A more civilised part wanted to stroke away her unhappiness. He certainly didn't want to be the cause of it. 'I just wanted you to see that we still had that. In case you were thinking...'

'I'm more than aware of our *compatibility*.' The word sounded so much uglier on her lips. Lea straightened. 'But it can't be part of my decision. If I stay, can you promise that we won't— That there'll be nothing physical between us? No pressure. No expectation?'

No. He couldn't promise that. Not when he burned with the need to touch her. But, if it wasn't what she wanted, then he didn't want it either. He wasn't completely devoid of pride.

Although you wouldn't know it these days.

'I give you my word I will never pressure you into anything, Lea.'

Her laugh was harsh, and entirely deserved. 'Forgive me if I struggle to believe that. You've done nothing but pressure me since I first came to Minamurra. Even tonight.'

It killed him that she was right. Is that how she saw him? 'I've wanted to hold you like that since Christmas.' His hand slipped unapologetically to her stomach. 'To feel my child growing in your body. To know that we have more than just weeks ahead of us.'

Ten...nine... The countdown started back in the barn. It seemed tragically appropriate.

'So, a new start for a new year?' he said.

Lea nodded sadly. 'Yes.'

'You'll stay? For good? As long as I don't touch you? We'll be a family?'

Six…five…

'Yes.' Her voice was barely a whisper; her single nod, tiny; her eyes utterly defeated. 'A family.'

He swept into her, pulling her to him and crushing her against his body. His mouth came down hard on hers, urgent, insistent, desperate to take the unhappiness away. Knowing it was likely the last time he'd taste her. She held herself ramrod-straight in his arms.

Three…two…

Then she sagged against him and let him in for the barest of heartbeats—into her hot, welcome passion—and kissed him the way he'd been dreaming of as a rousing New Year cheer went up in the distant barn. Angels burst into song somewhere.

She tore her lips from his and reeled back from him, betrayed. Wounded. Flushed with unmistakable passion.

The primitive part roared again. 'A new start for a new year,' he reminded her through a voice even he didn't recognise. 'That kiss was last year.'

And our last.

On that crushing thought, he turned and walked away from the woman who enthralled him, who had wheedled herself and her daughter so firmly into his heart. The woman he couldn't allow himself to want.

Back towards the party. Back to where a keg of beer and elective oblivion awaited.

Immunisation against a lifetime of not touching the woman he burned for.

CHAPTER TWELVE

MOLLY was weakening.

You could see it in the way that she played now: quieter, more reserved. In the way Max the Cat could pass through the living room without her doing more than reaching out to stroke his orange tail. The number of naps she now needed every day. The duration of her coughing attacks.

Death waited patiently for her in the shadows.

Dr Koek tweaked her medications, consulting long-distance and keeping Molly's body functioning chemically. Sounding more brightly positive each time. That artifice hit Lea the hardest. She caught herself hoping for a premature birth just so Molly's suffering could be eased sooner.

What kind of person did that make her?

Her chest was permanently tight throughout January. By February her blood pressure was up. Her appetite was down. Wanting Reilly and losing Molly was going to kill her, and there was nothing she could do about either.

'Hold on, baby,' she whispered to Molly during one of her many long naps. 'Just a few more weeks. You can make it. We both can.'

She turned to find Reilly watching her from the doorway, a strange expression in his eyes. He walked away without speaking.

Lea sighed. New Year's Eve had changed everything. A new, wary kind of tension that hadn't been there before now pulled everything tight between them. Like they needed any more hurdles in their relationship.

Their *business* relationship.

She rubbed her eyes. None of the pull that she'd felt six years ago had changed. It echoed in every conversation they had, it lurked in every encounter. Knowing he was also attracted only made the magnetic hum that much louder. Nine months of this had seemed doable. Endurable. Another fifty years was pressing down on her like a threat. Turning it off was the only way she was going to survive. By withdrawing.

She'd done harder things.

She closed the door on a sleeping Molly and padded towards the kitchen. It was empty. The living room, Reilly's study: both empty. She frowned and turned for the far end of the house. She knocked softly at the door to his bedroom suite, looking beyond the entryway into the masculine, beige-and-brown territory she'd never seen.

'Reilly?'

He stepped out of his *en suite* bathroom, his balled-up T-shirt in his hands, working jeans slung low on lean hips. His body was hardened by hard work instead of hours in a gym. She'd felt all that hardness pressed up against him on the dance floor. At the waterhole. In the kitchen.

Lord, that kiss felt like it was a lifetime ago.

He tossed the T-shirt across to the laundry hamper in a slam dunk and then looked back at Lea, his eyes guarded as they usually were these days. They dropped to her large belly and lingered there a moment, as though he had x-ray vision. Then they lifted back to hers. 'Is everything all right?'

She swallowed past her dry mouth. 'What time do we need to go?'

'The Valentine's rodeo starts at four, and it's a three-hour drive to Kununurra because the shortcut's washed out. Mrs Dawes is set to watch Molly from twelve. I'm just about to have a shower.' His eyes glittered as they watched her teeth worry her lip. 'Is there anything else?'

He reached for his belt and Lea flushed. Knowing it was her no-touching rule that made this scene such a joke didn't help make it funny. Reilly's casual state of undress screamed in the silence, testing the boundary she'd set. Testing them.

Withdraw.

She took a breath. 'I'm just worried about Molly. She's not well.'

Reilly stared at her for a long time, choosing his words carefully. 'She's been getting worse for weeks, Lea. Steadily. I don't think she'll suddenly crash, and if she does Mrs Dawes will call the Flying Doctor immediately. They've been briefed on her situation.'

Lea's chest crushed in painfully but she nodded, knowing it was true. Reilly had made sure all the emergency services had Molly's information. The Royal Flying Doctor Service was the most likely service to come for her. It was why they were here—the airstrip.

She'd do well to remember that.

'Or are you just looking for a reason to opt out? I won't force you to come.'

Lea studied him. Was she? 'No. I'd like to come. I'd like to understand you better.' Heat flooded her cheeks. Understand *it* better, she'd meant to say.

His eyes held hers, silent, as unforgiving as ever in these past, tense weeks.

Then his hands went back to his belt and unbuckled it with the economy of years of practice and it flew to the big bed with a decided snap. 'In that case, I'd better get cleaned up. I'll come for you just before noon.'

She heard his jeans unzip as he turned back to the bathroom. She spun round and hurried back down the hall, cheeks flaming.

The bathroom door clicked shut behind her, mocking her haste.

It wasn't what she'd expected. What she'd feared.

The particular rodeo fraternity that Reilly belonged to was more conscious of public expectation than others she'd heard of. Their event was family friendly; the horses and bulls won their rounds more often than the riders, which gave Lea a sense that it was a little more equal than she'd believed.

Reilly and a second pick-up rider were mounted for the whole event, glued to their saddles like they were born there. They cleared the arena between rides, ensuring the keyed-up bulls could find their way to the safety of the holding yards after they'd tossed their riders free. But their primary job was to pick up the bareback bronco-riders once they'd hit their eight seconds.

There was no good way off a suicide-ride bronco, so Reilly rode up hard next to the bucking, crazed horse long enough for the competitor to leap from the wild horse across the back of Reilly's bombproof one. Then they'd slide off the back, and Reilly and his partner would flank the wild-eyed bronco with their mounts so that it felt protected by the herd. Then they'd reach over and un-strap the binding tethers.

It calmed them instantly.

'Reilly!' Her hand shot to her mouth and silenced her accidental outburst. No one heard her under the cheering. She'd caught herself exclaiming much more for the pick-up teams and the hapless bulls than for the competitors themselves. If they wanted to maim themselves in the name of sport, they could go ahead. Riding pick-up seemed highly dangerous, but she could see the importance of the role. Reilly was not only responsible for the safety of the competitors but the welfare of the animals. Their contribution directly calmed the stressed livestock.

She struggled not to approve of that.

As she watched, Reilly cut a particularly recalcitrant bull into the holding area, finally ending its run around the arena; it snorted and bucked after the unprotected competitor threw himself over a barrier wall.

'And there goes Reilly Martin on his workhorse, Sprocket,' the announcer boomed into the PA system as Reilly slung the gate shut behind the bull. 'Nice work, mate. And nice horse, too. He breeds those himself out at Minamurra.'

The large crowd applauded as Reilly gave a humble wave of thanks for the plug, and Lea found herself unable to take her eyes off his confidence. The way he worked the horse with his legs, the stability of his seat, the teamwork between horse and rider; she wondered what he must have looked like competing in events but was glad he wouldn't be tonight. Her heart wouldn't be up to it.

Right on cue, Reilly glanced into the stands and found her with shielded eyes. She gave him a nervous smile. Not rude, but hardly encouraging. He looked away.

Damn.

Around her, hundreds of people were crammed into the public seating. Families, couples, singles on the prowl. It seemed like rodeo was a perfectly acceptable Valentine's activity in this part of the country. She let her eyes wander over the families, the husbands and wives, the partners. How many of them lived in marriages that were more about binding properties together, or settling for the nearest female, or surviving in harsh country? The bush seemed too sparse a place for every one of these people to have found the perfect love-match.

Maybe others out there had made the same kind of concession that she was making. For family.

Settling.

The thumping music increased in volume, signalling a break, and Lea knew the rodeo clowns would be back. The head clown performed for the kids in the crowd as, off to one side, new bulls were loaded into the six arena-chutes, awaiting their eight seconds of liberty.

The clown called three children from the crowd, none of them older than Molly, and had them out there with him now, solving a giant barrel-puzzle in the heart of the arena, going for the prize of a real-life cowboy hat. The three of them worked against the clock to win the hat, while the clanking of chute after chute being loaded with angry bulls was drowned out by the loud music.

Lea flicked her eyes to where Reilly lounged on horseback off to one side, taking a break until the pick-up team was needed again. Long display-chaps hung down from his hips, over his legs and stirrups, and fed the illusion that he was part of the horse. It was stupidly sexy. As if he needed any help with that.

Her heart thudded in time with the music.

Every eye in the place was on the activity in the centre of the arena, except Lea's. As if sensing her interest, Reilly turned and encountered her bold stare.

Hey.

Brown eyes held hers as his horse danced under him.

Hey yourself.

And then, barely consciously, her eye refocussed just past his shoulder, at the chute behind him being loaded with bulls. As she watched, a clamp in one of the chutes gave way to the pressure of one ton of angry bull slamming against it and, virtually in slow motion, the gate flung open into the arena, releasing an explosion of angry, bovine flesh.

Lea shot to her feet at the same time that she screamed Reilly's name.

He spun around, saw the disaster unfolding and then turned with Lea to look at the children standing unprotected in the centre of the arena. He dug his heels cruelly into Sprocket. Cattle hands leapt down off their chutes, and the head clown caught on just as Sprocket lurched into a standing gallop. The clown sprinted forward, slowed by his giant clown shoes, grabbed a child under each arm then bolted for the boundary fence. He practically threw them over into the arms of waiting strangers and leapt up onto the fence himself. He just didn't have enough arms for all three children.

Reilly bore down like a missile on the tiny, blond boy left standing frozen in the ring. So did the bull. The two animals raced for the centre of the arena, but Reilly got there first. The bull stopped to take its fury out on one of the empty barrels with his blunted horns and Reilly slid from the saddle, hanging by one hand on its pommel, and scooped the remaining child up into his arms. He righted himself and kicked the responsive Sprocket into high gear again.

The entire audience was on its feet, and several people screamed hysterically. Reilly galloped around the far side of the bull, keeping the child away from the feral animal, and his eyes hunted out Lea in the surging crowd.

She pushed forward.

He slammed Sprocket up against the barrier fence hard and hurled the screaming child towards her even as her arms reached out. There was no time for something gentler. Adrenaline gave her the strength to catch the flailing boy and fold him into her arms as though he were Molly, rocking and soothing him as only a mother could.

As she rocked, her eyes sought Reilly out in the arena, her heart thundering painfully. He was circling the bull, letting it burn off some of its aggression on the hapless barrels. The prized cowboy-hat lay crushed in the red dirt, trampled by massive hooves. Four clowns and the other pick-up guy got in on the act and worked with Reilly to encourage the panicked bull back into the holding yard, which now stood wide open. Someone released other steers into the arena and they immediately formed a small herd, drawing the overwhelmed animal into their centre. Reilly worked the herd like he'd worked the brumbies, cutting them back and round until all five of them obediently trotted through the exit gate to the holding yards.

As it swung shut, a blonde woman crashed headlong into Lea and the boy in her arms, tearing him from her careful hold, a mother's tears streaming down her face.

Lea felt her own start to run at what they'd all just witnessed, the deathly disaster they'd very nearly had. She thought immediately of Molly.

Her streaming eyes lifted to the arena. Reilly leaned stiffly down from his horse to a group of officials who'd gathered around the broken chute, and whatever he said had impact because one of them nodded, looked to the announcer's box and cut his flattened hand across his throat. Loud music burst into life and waiting competitors stood down from their positions.

The rodeo was over.

Sprocket's eyes were white and rolling and his glossy coat was now flecked with foam as Reilly walked him back across the arena. He patted the horse's neck reassuringly and then cut a direct course for Lea, lifting stricken eyes to hers.

She didn't hesitate.

She clambered to the front row of the tiered seating that

looked down over the sunken arena and pressed her body over
the barrier. Reilly threw down the reins and turned the horse
against the barrier with his legs. Without thinking, Lea, threw
her arms around him, her feet practically leaving the stadium
seats, and she buried her face in his neck. He stank of sweat
and horse and fear. But she held on for dear life.

He slid his arms up to hold her, steady her, and wrapped
them hard around her body. Both of them were shaking. She
wasn't yet capable of speech, only action. Right now, in this
moment, she didn't care how hard she'd worked to keep him
at a distance, the pledge she'd made him give. She only knew
that she'd felt the same gut-tearing fear when Reilly was in
danger as she felt for Molly. The fear of losing someone she...

Oh, God. Realisation battered her like the bull's horns on a
barrel.

She loved Reilly Martin. Desperately and entirely, despite
every precaution she'd taken. Despite knowing she was just a
means to an end for him. Knowing that he didn't love her back.

She took his face in both her hands and then kissed him as
though it was her child he'd just saved. Her body thrilled at the
double rush of adrenaline and pure foolish, misguided love, her
heart bursting with the ache. A dull kind of sickness spread through
her as she realised what she had to do. What loving him meant.

She worshipped him with her mouth. Kissing him as though
it was the very last time she ever would.

She was absolutely certain it would be.

CHAPTER THIRTEEN

'Okay, Lea?' Reilly's concerned eyes moved between her and the drenched road ahead.

Her misery doubled, but she faked a smile and a nod. 'Just tired.'

The rain had started again when they were an hour out of Kununurra. Reilly's battered old Land Rover was comfortable and solid, and he mastered it and the horse trailer with supreme confidence through the wet. Lea stared out into the darkness and let the rain drumming on the roof lull her into a half-sleep. She twisted against the ache in her body caused by two close encounters with a steel barrier.

Reilly's eyes returned to the road.

How could she have done it? Not the kissing; that had just been pure gut-reaction. A release of endorphins and tension from their near miss. And God knew it was hard to regret something that felt that good. That right.

It was what lay behind the kissing that disturbed her. She'd been so terrified for Reilly, certain in that moment that she was going to lose another person that she... The sick feeling swelled back up. Another person she *loved*—love, not attraction. Not affection. The real McCoy.

She loved him despite his terrible cockiness, his fondness for taking charge, his long history of empty relationships. She loved him because of his essential goodness, his tenderness. His heartbreakingly beautiful smile.

She squeezed her eyes shut.

How could this happen? He'd forced her to sign over her child to him. He'd put conditions on the saving of Molly's life. She'd resigned herself to that, had decided it was survivable, because of Molly. She would endure. Giving up the child was her price to pay.

Then he'd handed her the miracle she'd been waiting for—the chance to stay together. To be a family.

A deep hollowness opened up in her chest like a cavern collapsing. Pain rushed in to fill the void. She'd spent over twenty years waiting for her father's love, trying to earn it, never being quite worthy. Could she really do the same for the rest of her life with the feelings she had for Reilly? Knowing he was only with her because she came as part of the family package?

Knowing she faced a lifetime of unreturned love?

It would eat her up. But if she didn't stay... She pressed the heel of her hand to her left breast to stop her heart haemorrhaging.

'Why don't you try and get some sleep?' Concerned, dark eyes were on her again.

He still worried about her, despite everything she'd done to him. Everything she'd said at New Year. He was a good man with so much to offer a child, the right woman, no matter what hurdles she set up in front of him. Reilly deserved his chance at fatherhood. She couldn't bear the idea of banishing him to the place he feared the most: a life of loneliness. He'd spent his one chance of fatherhood on saving Molly. Which meant she just couldn't keep the baby she was carrying. His baby.

The haemorrhage widened out to become a swollen ache in her chest. She pressed harder. They had a contract. More importantly, she could never bring herself to do that to him.

The ache moved south into her gut. Her hand slid to her belly. But that meant giving birth to this little life and then handing it over, pretending it had never existed. Could she wind back the clock nine months? Go back to how it was before she'd driven down Minamurra's long, tree-lined driveway?

Just mother and daughter. Except Molly would be robust and healthy, whereas she...

She would never be quite whole again.

But she would survive. She always did. She took a deep breath, knowing what had to be done.

'Reilly?'

He looked at her. Those brown eyes ate into her resolve like acid. This was the best way. A tiny hint of sweat broke out on her skin. 'What happened tonight…'

'Lea, that never should have happened. There'll be a formal investigation. Rodeo's not normally like that.'

His unexpected response dented her momentum. She blinked.

He took his focus from the road to glance at her speculatively. 'But that's not what we're talking about?'

The guarded expression in his eyes hit her low and hard. She squirmed against the sensation. 'No.'

'You're talking about the kiss?'

Close enough. It was somewhere to start. She'd kissed him as though they were making love on horseback. 'I shouldn't have done that. It wasn't fair.'

'On who? Did you hear me complaining?'

No, he hadn't complained. He'd kissed her back as if she were pure oxygen. Her voice cracked. 'You're a good person, Reilly. I don't want to end up hurting you. Hating you.'

His hands stiffened on the steering wheel. 'Why would you do that?'

The windscreen wipers swished back and forth in time with her pulse. She winced as a pang of regret stabbed through her, low and hard. 'I can't do it, Reilly. I can't stay for ever.' She saw his face grey in front of her. 'I need to leave once the baby's born.'

A muscle ticked high in his jaw. 'We had an agreement.'

'I'll honour the contract.'

'Forget the contract.' He slammed the steering wheel in frustration. 'I thought we'd agreed, between us, that you would stay. You thought about it long enough.'

'I didn't…' *know I loved you then* '…think the ramifications through.'

Poisoned pain spat from his eyes. 'Seems to be the story of

your life, Lea. Now you're wanting out of a relationship after just a few weeks.'

Hurt slashed through her. 'It's not a relationship, Reilly, it's an arrangement. Don't you want more?'

Brown eyes blazed. 'Damn right I want more. But we don't always get what we want.'

The truth of that stabbed her sharply. Twice. In close succession. Lea frowned. 'Reilly…'

'You're running from this because you're afraid you don't know how to *be* a family, Lea. You've isolated yourself for so long.'

Her frown grew into a wince as more pain sliced across her abdomen. Only part of it was her heart rupturing. Her hand curled around the door handle.

No… 'Reilly…'

'I'm prepared to put up with a lot, Lea, in the interests of our children having a proper family. But I'm not going to beg.'

'*Reilly!*' Her sharp tone finally got his attention. His mouth snapped shut and he glared at her. She took a deep breath and spoke with a shaky voice. 'I think I'm in labour.'

The anger fell from his face along with all the blood. 'But it's too soon.'

Lea pushed herself up off the seat to ease another spasm. It was all very familiar. Molly had started this way, except weeks later in the pregnancy. Her heart pounded. 'Thank you for pointing out the obvious. Shall I convince him to go back in?'

Reilly cursed and then swung the vehicle and horse trailer to the side of the road. He turned back to her immediately, reaching for his satellite phone. 'You'll be okay, Lea. We're closer to the hospital here than if you'd gone into labour at Minamurra.'

The quiet confidence in his voice reassured her momentarily. Then another spasm ripped through her belly. She groaned. It shouldn't be that soon.

'Please, no…'

Her whispered plea filled the car. They both knew the c sequences if anything went wrong with this pregnancy baby, no stem cells.

No stem cells, no Molly.

No Molly. A tiny voice whispered through that terrible fear; no Molly, and there would be no reason in the world for Reilly and Lea to remain in each other's lives.

'Ambulance, please,' Reilly barked into the phone, never taking his eyes off Lea. 'Hurry.'

Lea forced back tears. How did a woman who thought she had nothing suddenly find herself with so much to lose?

He drove back towards Kununurra like he was leading a stampede. They met the ambulance halfway; the paramedics transferred Lea into it immediately and assessed her condition.

It was definitely labour. Six weeks early.

They admitted Lea to hospital, doubled over with pain and wet, alone and frightened. Reilly had fallen behind the racing ambulance in the rain, pulling a trailer, but she was sure he would come. Despite everything.

He would come.

'Is there anyone we can call, Ms Curran?' The receiving nurse noted her near-hysterical condition. Lea gave them Dr Koek's number and Anna's. She could really use one of her sisters now. Maybe both.

'Our staff are aware of the need to preserve your cord and placenta,' the nurse told her efficiently, still filling out admission information. 'Our lab has been sent the equipment we need and, um, we're just getting it all set up. We weren't expecting you this soon.'

Oh, God. 'The baby?' Lea whimpered.

'Is early but not critically so. Premature bubs do really well these days, don't worry.' She seemed so sure. But six weeks… The nurse scribbled more information on the clipboard as they wheeled Lea straight through to Emergency. 'Did you sustain an injury in the past few days? A knock to the baby?'

Lea stared. The barrier fence. The child. The blonde woman. They'd all slammed into her. 'Today? A child was—'

The nurse cut her off, not caring for details. 'What kind of ? Fall? Impact?'

'Impact?' Lea stuttered. Had she hurt her baby leaping into Reilly's arms? Only hours ago she'd selfishly wished the baby would come early.

Oh, God...

'Lea.'

Relief washed through her. She twisted around. 'Reilly.'

He was crouched by her side in a moment. The passing nurses looked enviously at the handsome man racing to his love's side. *If only they knew.*

'What's going on?' Reilly's imperious request got much more response than her own whispered questions. He was back by her ear in moments. 'They're preparing Theatre just in case, Lea. And the lab, for the stem cells. But they're going to try and stop the labour.'

'Molly?'

'Mrs Dawes is going to sit with her all night. She's asleep. She's fine.'

Tears welled on her lashes. She gripped his hand. 'It's too early, Reilly.'

He didn't waste his breath with platitudes. 'I know.'

'I didn't mean to hurt the baby.' The tears spilled over.

'Shh.' He kissed her forehead. 'I know.'

'What I said, in the car...' The last syllable was elongated as a contraction hit Lea square in the mid-section. She doubled over on a moan. Reilly held her through it, looking about helplessly for someone to come and help. Despite the pain, she grabbed his chin and pulled his eyes back to hers.

'I need you to know.' Her voice was tight. 'I will honour our agreement. Even though I'm not staying. I want you to take the baby, Reilly.'

'Lea...'

She clutched his fingers. 'We had an agreement.'

Confusion and disbelief wracked his beautiful face. 'You would give up your child rather than be with me?'

'You say that like it's an easy choice. I *can't* stay with you Reilly. I don't want to end up hating you.'

Because you can't love me back.

Her heart wrenched with spasms as painful as her labour. Tears began to flow.

'Don't try and talk, Lea. Just tell me one thing—one word; I know you won't lie.' He swallowed and brushed strands of damp hair back from her face, talking thickly. 'Could you love me? In time?'

Every thread in every muscle of her body screamed at her to say yes. Independent of her will, they started coordinating themselves in a series of microscopic contractions that forced her lips into the right shape for a 'yes'. She forced them closed as yet another lightning bolt of pain ripped through her. She bared her teeth in a savage snarl that was about so much more than being in labour.

If she said yes he'd only persuade her, charm her, seduce her into compliance. He'd promise her anything if it meant having the family he so desperately wanted. And, stupid fool that she was, she'd believe him. Until next time something happened to remind her that she was in this alone. That her love was one-sided. Sacrificing herself to a loveless marriage would only lead her to resent Reilly. And Molly. And the new baby. Pain flowed down her cheeks.

She couldn't lie. And she couldn't tell him the truth. She turned her streaming eyes to his.

I love you with everything in me. 'You're getting the baby, Reilly. That has to be enough. I'm so sorry.'

He stumbled to his feet, ashen.

Out of nowhere, nursing staff swarmed in and pulled Lea away and down the corridor. Others followed her with machines on wheels. 'You'll need to wait here,' one of them told him gently. And then Lea was gone.

Reilly's world spun around him.

I'm so sorry...

Sorry that she couldn't imagine herself loving him, even for the sake of her children? She'd give up a baby rather than be with him? His gut ached like he was sharing the pain of her labour, the physical price of bringing their baby into the world.

He would gladly take it on, and more, if it spared Lea the agony he'd seen in her eyes.

I want you to take the baby...

Hurt and anger mixed in an excruciating alchemy, bubbled up in his blood, drove him out into the ambulance receiving-area. He swore. He never should have pressured Lea to stay. She wasn't ready. He'd pushed too hard, consumed with his dream to have a picture-book family, to give his children the upbringing he'd never had: a father and mother around all the time, a happy, stable family home. He'd forced her hand using the baby as bait.

Exactly like his mother had with his father.

The pain froze his breath. A siren wailed somewhere in the night. Icy awareness rattled through him and he grabbed the edge of the still-warm ambulance for support.

Adele Martin had manipulated her husband into a lifetime together. Her son had done the same with Lea. His heart pitched and he struggled for breath.

He was made in his mother's image.

Kevin Martin had loved Adele secretly for years. He'd gone willingly, blindly, into their marriage only to discover one person's love couldn't sustain them both. Eventually, he'd turned numb just to survive. He would go to his grave knowing the woman he loved had never truly loved him. He was living his long, miserable life that way.

Reilly closed his eyes and rested his forehead on the ambulance.

Lea was right. They'd end up hating each other the way he suspected his parents did. His feelings for her wouldn't be enough. And Molly and the new baby wouldn't be any more oblivious to the undercurrents than Reilly had been as a child.

He would not be responsible for inflicting that on another child.

'Mr Martin?' A nurse shouted from the hospital doorway. Reilly snapped his burning eyes toward her. She backed up a step. 'They've not been able to stop the labour. We're prepping the theatre for a C-section.'

His heart hammered against his ribs. Surgery. His son or

daughter would be born tonight, for better or for worse. The fantasy family of the past months was over. Lea wouldn't be staying. Molly wouldn't be staying. He knew in his heart that he couldn't take this new child from Lea or Molly, contract or no contract.

His family was finished.

He turned and walked into the darkness.

'Mr Martin…?'

A dull cloak settled back over his heart, muffling the pain as he stumbled down to the car park. Reilly recognised the sensation the moment it returned: the numbness that had got him through his childhood. His father's numbness.

He barely heard the confused nurse call him a third time.

He hadn't realised the deadened sheath had lifted at all. But he saw it clearly now, blowing up and away when Lea had walked up his stairs that first day.

Maybe the survival anaesthesia would take him through his life just as it had his father. He slid the metaphorical cloak back on, retried it for size—Reilly Martin, king of the circuit. Heart of stone. Untouchable.

It fit so snugly he didn't even feel the rain as he walked stiffly off towards the darkness of his future.

Alone.

CHAPTER FOURTEEN

'GOOD morning, Mummy.'

Clammy hands touched her face sweetly, drawing her out of a deep, exhausted sleep. She struggled to sit up.

Molly?

'Shh. Just relax, Lea.' Warmth from a second touch spread through Lea as the soft voice and smell of apples trickled into her consciousness.

'Anna?' She scanned the room through groggy eyes: no Reilly. Her heart sank. Why was she surprised?

'I'm here. Molly's here. You're going to be fine, Lea.'

She'd come. Anna was in a hospital, the place she hated above all others. 'Jared?'

'We're leaving for India next week. Jared's getting everything ready; he sends his love.'

Love. The closest she'd be getting to it, anyway, the platonic affection of a brother-in-law. Lea pushed herself to a sitting position. The ache of emptiness in her lower body and the pull of surgical staples reminded her of why they were here. Her eyes flew open.

'The baby...'

Creases formed between Anna's blue eyes, concerned. Confused. But there for her. 'He's doing fine, Lea. He's small, but everything works. He's breathing on his own.'

Invisible fists squeezed her heart painfully. *A boy.*

Reilly had a son.

'Why won't you see him, Lea?' Anna's voice was low, conscious of Molly now playing in the hallway with someone else's little girl.

Avoidance. 'The stem cells?'

Anna's lips tightened, not fooled. 'On their way to Perth. He was a good match.'

Tears sprang into both their eyes. They both knew what that meant for Molly.

'Your son, Lea. Why won't you…?'

'Not *my* son.' She knew her tone was bleak, knew she should be pulling herself out of it, but unable to. *'Reilly's.'*

Anna stared at her silently, assessing. Then she changed tack. 'Reilly. Now he's an interesting one. He looks just like Molly.'

The tears spilled over. 'You've met him?'

Anna nodded, folding a tissue into Lea's cold fingers. 'He's here. He brought Molly in first thing.'

Lea's heart squeezed. Here—but not *here*.

'He called us late last night. Asked us to come.' Anna was relentless when she wanted something. Lea studied the dull, beige room. Anna leaned closer, a glint in her eye. 'He's very good-looking.'

Lea smiled, though it was weak. The sisters had grown up with a similar eye for quality males. It had been something of a hobby in their younger years. Back before life got serious.

The glint evaporated. 'Your baby needs you, Lea.'

Lea knew exactly how difficult this would be for Anna. Babies. Hospitals. She loved her husband but she had a raw place in her heart that was forever reserved for the baby she'd lost. A boy.

She blinked furiously. 'God, Anna.'

Just like that, strong arms were around her and Lea felt the familiar screen of toffee-coloured silk drape around them. Anna's hair smelt of sunshine and straw. Lea's tears tumbled.

Anna's voice was raw, pained. 'You need to see him. He needs his mother.'

'I can't. I can't look at him.'

'He needs to feed, Lea. He needs you.'

'I'll express.' She stumbled on. 'Or formula. I can't get close. He's not mine to love.'

She told Anna about her arrangement with Reilly, pausing to breathe raggedly between tears.

Anna's blue eyes widened with disbelief. Her long fingers shook. 'You signed that?'

Shame speared through Lea. 'It was for Molly.' Her eyes dropped. 'I would have signed anything.'

Blue fire crackled under a deep frown. 'And Reilly wants this? Wants to take your child away?'

Lea immediately fired up, fierce, ferocious. 'He has as much right to this baby as I do. It was part of our agreement. He needs it.'

Anna stared at her, eyes wide.

Lea bristled. 'What?'

'You love him.'

Lea swallowed. Sudden tension filled the room.

'You love him enough to give your baby up. Oh, my God.'

Lea broke, hot and angry. 'Don't say it like that. Is it such a surprise that I know how to love?'

'Oh, Lea. No.' Anna hurried to fix her gaffe. 'I just... I had no idea.'

Me, neither.

'God, it must have been so hard all these months. You were made to love someone, Lea Curran. Someone worthy.'

'He is worthy,' she whispered.

'But?'

Lea breathed in deep. 'But he doesn't love me. He likes me.' Her laugh was a shade hysterical. 'He's attracted to me.' Her voice softened and she pressed her hand, complete with IV drip attachments, to her pained heart. 'He really loves Molly.'

Both women glanced out at the dark-haired poppet in the hall. She looked up and smiled brilliantly through deathly pale lips: Reilly's smile.

'What's not to love?' Anna whispered. 'And he still want this baby? He's said that?'

Lea frowned. 'I signed a contract.'

'Months ago, Lea. What about recently?'

She gingerly told her about Reilly's proposition that they be a family. Anna's eyes saddened, Lea's eyes prickled dangerously again.

'You need to talk to him, Lea. He's right outside.'

She shook her head. 'I can't. I've hurt him too much.'

'You've hurt *him*?'

'He wanted this so badly. A family. He deserves a real one.'

Anna frowned. 'But you love him. Molly loves him. How is that not real?'

Had motherhood turned Anna obtuse? 'He doesn't love me, Anna.'

Anna watched her carefully. 'So?'

The fists squeezed again. Critically hard. 'Am I the only one who believes I'm worthy of being loved? Is it so unrealistic? First Dad, then Reilly, now you.'

Anna's head came up. 'How long are you planning on wallowing in that, Lea? How many lives are you going to mess up because you had a terrible relationship with our father?'

Lea felt her sister's brutal words like a slap across the jaw.

Anna barrelled on passionately. 'Dad made a lot of mistakes. He wasn't perfect. He was just a man; he lost his way when he lost the woman who gave him strength. He had to raise two tiny daughters in man's country and he didn't have a clue where to start.' She leaned in closer. 'You were older, so he did all his learning on you. By the time Sapphie and I came along, he'd already worked out what didn't work through trial and error. Mostly error, I'll concede.'

She stared at her sister.

'You showed him, Lea. Over and over. Every day he knew he'd messed up with you, and you never forgave him.' Her eyes dropped. 'I can't imagine how hard that must have been for you, keeping his secret, but I can imagine how it must have een for him. How much shame he carried around, knowing at you knew. That you judged him. He would have seen it ry time he looked in your eyes.'

Lea swallowed past the large lump in her throat. 'Jared told you.'

'Yes, he did.'

'You think it's my fault?'

'No, Lea. It is what it is. But you can't let the past destroy things in the present. Affect Molly. Affect your son. You need to break the cycle.'

Lea rubbed confused eyes. 'You think I should stay with Reilly despite the fact he doesn't love me? How is that better for Molly? What lessons would she learn from that?'

'No. I agree you can't do that. I did it for five years before Jared and I worked it all out, and it nearly broke me. But if you're leaving you need to tell him why. From what you've told me, he could benefit from knowing someone loved him, too.'

A cold fist tightened around Lea's intestines.

Anna stood stiffly, her eyes glittering dangerously. 'And then one of you needs to step up for that little boy. Someone needs to hold him and love him. I don't care which of you it is; he's already gone too many hours with only the nursing staff to cling to.'

Anna walked out as Lea burst into tears.

'Lea? Anna said you needed me.'

Bloody Anna. But even as she thought it, Lea knew it was unfair. Anna was the only one working for their baby right now. Shame washed through her.

'Lea, don't cry.' Reilly sank down onto the bed next to her, tired, cautious. 'Everything will be okay.'

'Have you seen him?' Lea asked, swiping at the escaped tears. She needed to know something about her baby. His mother's hair or his father's? Whose eyes? Everything where it should be?

Reilly studied the bed linen. 'No.'

Lea's face came up. 'Why not?'

His eyes were unreadable. 'I've destroyed the contract, L I'm not going to take him from you. From his sister.'

Her stomach contracted painfully.

'A family should stay together. I won't be respons'
pulling one apart. The nurses are bringing him up to yo

It was all happening so fast. It was what she wanted—of course it was—but not at any cost. The cost of Reilly's heart. She could see the pain etched into his features. He was giving up two children.

'Reilly, what about Molly? The baby?'

'I'm going to go before he comes in; it's the easiest way. I don't think I can see him just yet. I just wanted to say goodbye. We'll talk by phone about maybe sorting out access visits. I want to see them both, sometimes.'

A rock-ball of emotion lodged in her chest. This was it, the thought of never seeing Reilly again. Or, worse, seeing him once a year on Molly's birthday, still loving him. Seeing him every day in the smiles of her children. Suddenly, that seemed a very real possibility.

He stood, his eyes heavily shielded. 'Good luck, Lea. You deserve to be happy. Tell Molly I'll ring her.' He gently kissed her forehead and walked out of the room. Out of her life.

The heart-rate monitor hooked up to her went berserk.

'Reilly!'

His footsteps disappeared down the hall.

'God damn you, Reilly Martin.' The furious curse helped power her up. She struggled free of the covers on the bed and swung her legs over the side, wincing as the row of surgical staples bit savagely into her flesh. The cables connecting her to a half-dozen monitoring devices tangled like parachute cords as she tried to remove them. In the end she ripped all but the IV drip off her skin and threw them to the floor. Her skin bled where the fixings should be.

The wheeled stand holding the IV-drip proved a terrific walking stick and she used it to haul herself onto shaky legs and propel herself out the door as the heart monitor went into alarm behind her. A concerned nurse tried to intercept her but pushed past with a brisk apology.

Her flimsy hospital gown fluttered open at the back but she care. The whole world could look at her naked butt if it tching up with Reilly.

uldn't let him walk away thinking he wasn't loved by

someone, no matter how humiliating for her. She'd been doing things the easiest way for too long.

The automatic doors opened out into the hospital car-park that was awash with seasonal rain. The cool splatter immediately hit her. 'Reilly.'

He turned, far across the car park, and sprinted back towards her when he saw her lurching out, unprotected, into the rain. Her heart thumped like a drum, high on adrenaline and thrilling one last time at the sight of his powerful body coming towards her. In seconds she was drenched, her light gown slaked to her naked skin, covering nothing. Her staples pulled painfully too.

She didn't care about either.

Reilly peeled off his jacket as he got closer and wrapped it around her, pulling her close to him. 'Are you trying to kill yourself, Lea?'

His voice was furious but his body was warm and familiar. And like home. That didn't make this any easier.

Warm rain poured down on them both. Reilly's body and thick oilskin coat shielded her from the worst of it. It was such a beautiful, tragic metaphor for their whole relationship. Would anyone ever protect her like this again? She pushed the thought away.

'I'm sorry, Reilly. I'm sorry I can't stay.' She appealed up into dark eyes. 'I don't want you to be alone...'

He shook his head, shutters dropping on those beautiful eyes. 'It's not your problem, Lea. I'm not some kind of charity case.'

She bled for the pain in his voice. She could hear the child behind the man. 'I know how it feels, Reilly. It's why I kept Molly.' She shivered even though the rain wasn't cold. He pulled the coat tighter around her. 'I told myself all kinds of things. Justified going ahead with the pregnancy a hundred ways. But I did it for selfish reasons, because I wasn't strong enough to be alone. I should have been stronger.'

Her eyes fell from his and touched on his lips before sett' somewhere around his throat. 'I'm trying to be strong now, F I'm trying to do the right thing, not the easiest thing. Stayi you would be so easy. But, in time, it would only hurt b

He lifted her chin with a gentle finger. His gaze was tragic. 'I know, Lea. I understand.'

'No, you don't.' She took a breath as rain trickled down her face, over her lips. 'Staying is so seductive because I could see you every day, smell you, watch you with our daughter. Our son.' Her voice broke on that one. 'I've even caught myself thinking—just for a nanosecond—that if our baby wasn't a match for Molly I'd get to stay with you longer.' Her heart bled. 'What kind of person does that make me?'

Reilly shook his head but she rushed on. 'But, ultimately, staying would kill me. I love you, Reilly, but I need to be loved back.'

His eyes flared like her wild horses', and he opened his mouth to speak. Lea cut him off. 'I can't go back on my commitment to myself. Even though it's hurting you. I'm so sorry.'

She let her head fall forward to rest on the strength of his chest. She felt his words rumbling in his body as much as heard them. His hand came up to thread through her saturated hair. His strength rushed into the vacuum within her.

'You're leaving because I don't love you?'

She lifted her face back to his scowling one. 'I'm not trying to blame you. I just want you to know why I'm leaving. I wondered if just knowing I *could* love someone would be enough, because I was seriously starting to wonder, but it's not. I want to be loved, Reilly. I need to be loved. I know that seems weak.'

His smile was bittersweet and he stroked her wet hair from her face, shaking his head. 'It's not weak.'

She blazed up at him. 'I want you to know you will always be welcome in your children's lives.' *No matter how hard that will be.* 'We'll work something out.'

His stare was intense. Finally he spoke. 'It's not enough, Lea.' The air sucked out of her and she stumbled a pace back. 'hat?'

'nowing I have a family somewhere, seeing them occasion-
's not enough. I want the whole package. I deserve more
ghter. Son. Wife.' He blazed down at her. 'People to love.'
ook her head. Had he not heard her? 'Reilly…'

'People I *already* love,' he clarified.

Daughter. Son. Lea gasped.

Wife.

'You love Molly.'

'I love you both, Lea.'

The ground shifted beneath her and she clung half to Reilly, half to the IV drip. He held her up at the elbows. Intense heat rained down on her from his eyes, warming her chilled body.

'I've loved you since you rode wild with the brumbies.' He risked a fleeting kiss on her frigid lips. Warmth leached out from the contact. 'It took me a while to recognise the sensation.'

He loved her? She became aware of the nursing staff hovering anxiously with umbrellas. She clung to Reilly. *Not yet.* She wasn't ready to be away from him.

Her voice broke. 'You love me?'

'So much it hurts. I thought you'd guessed. Weren't we talking about that when we came in yesterday?'

'I thought we were talking about me. My feelings.'

Reilly groaned and pulled her against his lips. 'We're going to have to talk more.'

Lea clung to him. 'I thought you just wanted a family. Badly enough to take me too.'

His angry growl was answer enough. 'I didn't want just *any* family. I wanted *this* family. I wanted you.'

'You wanted the baby.'

He nodded. 'I did, at the beginning. But I could have just turned up on delivery day and taken him if that's what it was really all about. I wanted you, Lea. And Molly. I love *you.*'

His scorching mouth bled heat into hers, a crazy, thrilling kind of life support. She pressed herself to her toes to feed on his strong, full lips. Then he pulled away, his voice a smooth tumble of river stones. 'Unless you can think of any reason that t[...] people who love each other can't be together, then I really, [...] badly, would like to marry you, Lea Curran. If you'll hav[...]

Lea held her stitches together as she stretched up to [...] mouth again, pressing a dozen acceptances into h[...] mouth, laughing and crying all at once. His ha[...]

around behind her to tuck the open folds of the saturated gown more modestly together. She felt him smile against her lips.

'We need to get you inside without anyone else seeing you,' he whispered. 'Bad enough that I'm ogling the wet body of a woman who's just had surgery.'

Lea laughed and slipped her arms into the sleeves of his coat, sliding it on properly. The movement temporarily revealed the pink flush of her breasts, rounded and aching with milk, through the translucence of the wet hospital gown.

Reilly's eyes darkened further. He blew out a steadying breath and nodded to the hospital entrance. 'It seems impossible, but I think there's someone inside who needs those even more than I do.'

A nurse darted forward and pointedly handed Reilly a large umbrella then sprinted back into the cover of the foyer. He steadied Lea's IV-drip as she turned, curled in his embrace, and limped barefoot back into the hospital towards their daughter. And their new son.

The rain poured on.

EPILOGUE

BABY Harrison certainly had a decent set of choppers on him. Lea winced as the emerging teeth grated on the sensitive flesh of her breast as he hungrily fed. She shifted on the comfortable swing-chair on Minamurra's wide veranda as the fabulous June sunshine sprinkled down on them.

Definitely time for solids. That would disappoint the little man in her arms, but she knew an older one who'd be delighted to have exclusive access at long last. She smiled at the thought. Her eyes found Reilly out in the left paddock, working one of the heavily pregnant mares in broad circles. Without the distraction of a hot-blooded stallion prancing about the place looking for trouble, the females had settled down well, showing Reilly what an intelligent and bombproof breed the brumbies were.

He had two orders for new-blood foals that weren't even conceived yet.

Frank Dawes had trucked God's Gift back to his mob at Yurraji, and then he'd trucked his wife and forty boxes of lord-knew-what out there. They were to become caretakers. Agnes had been only too happy to hang up her apron after a lifetime of caring for Reilly, and Frank had finally felt ready to call love of his life 'wife' in the true sense and live with her. A ripe age of sixty-two.

They were as happy as clams in her grandfather's lit

Lea swapped Harrison to the other breast and s into the cushions. Life was good. Despite the bes

Adele, the nightmare mother-in-law, their wedding had been simple, homely and crawling with children—Liam and Sapphie's Harry, and Anna and Jared's surprise sisters from India. Lea had caught Reilly clearing his throat thickly a number of times as he'd looked around him in dazed appreciation of the crowded, crazy family he was about to join.

Not that he had a moment's doubt, as he reminded her in very tangible terms every evening.

She stretched in satisfaction. Yes, putting two loners together had worked out pretty well. Very well, in fact.

Max the cat sprinted wildly across the house-paddock, a squealing Molly in hot pursuit. Molly with the flushed, pink cheeks and salmon-coloured lips of perfect, miraculous health. Lea caught herself as she was about to call out, 'Walk!'

She swallowed back a lump and let her daughter run.

Coming Next Month

Available July 13, 2010

#4177 A WISH AND A WEDDING
Margaret Way and Melissa James

#4178 THE BRIDESMAID'S SECRET
Fiona Harper
The Brides of Bella Rosa

#4179 MAID FOR THE MILLIONAIRE
Susan Meier
Housekeepers Say I Do!

#4180 SOS: CONVENIENT HUSBAND REQUIRED
Liz Fielding

#4181 VEGAS PREGNANCY SURPRISE
Shirley Jump
Girls' Weekend in Vegas

#4182 WINNING A GROOM IN 10 DATES
Cara Colter
The Fun Factor

LARGER-PRINT BOOKS!
GET 2 FREE LARGER-PRINT NOVELS PLUS
2 FREE GIFTS!

HARLEQUIN® *Romance*®

From the Heart, For the Heart

YES! Please send me 2 FREE LARGER-PRINT Harlequin® Romance novels and my 2 FREE gifts (gifts are worth about $10). After receiving them, if I don't wish to receive any more books, I can return the shipping statement marked "cancel." If I don't cancel, I will receive 6 brand-new novels every month and be billed just $4.07 per book in the U.S. or $4.47 per book in Canada. That's a saving of at least 22% off the cover price! It's quite a bargain! Shipping and handling is just 50¢ per book.* I understand that accepting the 2 free books and gifts places me under no obligation to buy anything. I can always return a shipment and cancel at any time. Even if I never buy another book from Harlequin, the two free books and gifts are mine to keep forever.

186/386 HDN E5N4

Name   (PLEASE PRINT)

Address   Apt. #

City   State/Prov.   Zip/Postal Code

Signature (if under 18, a parent or guardian must sign)

Mail to the **Harlequin Reader Service:**
IN U.S.A.: P.O. Box 1867, Buffalo, NY 14240-1867
IN CANADA: P.O. Box 609, Fort Erie, Ontario L2A 5X3

Not valid for current subscribers to Harlequin Romance Larger-Print books.

Are you a current subscriber to Harlequin Romance books and want to receive the larger-print edition? Call 1-800-873-8635 today!

* Terms and prices subject to change without notice. Prices do not include applicable taxes. N.Y. residents add applicable sales tax. Canadian residents will be charged applicable provincial taxes and GST. Offer not valid in Quebec. This offer is limited to one order per household. All orders subject to approval. Credit or debit balances in a customer's account(s) may be offset by any other outstanding balance owed by or to the customer. Please allow 4 to 6 weeks for delivery. Offer available while quantities last.

Your Privacy: Harlequin Books is committed to protecting your privacy. Our Privacy Policy is available online at www.eHarlequin.com or upon request from the Reader Service. From time to time we make our lists of customers available to reputable third parties who may have a product or service of interest to you. ☐ you would prefer we not share your name and address, please check here.

Help us get it right—We strive for accurate, respectful and relevant communications. To clarify or modify your communication preferences, visit us at www.ReaderService.com/consumerschoice.

HRLP10R

HARLEQUIN®

A *Romance*

FOR EVERY MOOD™

Spotlight on
Heart & Home

Heartwarming romances
where love can happen
right when you least expect it.

See the next page to enjoy a sneak peek
from Silhouette Special Edition®,
a Heart and Home series.

Introducing McFARLANE'S PERFECT BRIDE
by USA TODAY *bestselling author Christine Rimmer,*
from Silhouette Special Edition®.

Entranced. Captivated. Enchanted.

Connor sat across the table from Tori Jones and couldn't help thinking that those words exactly described what effect the small-town schoolteacher had on him. He might as well stop trying to tell himself he wasn't interested. He was powerfully drawn to her.

Clearly, he should have dated more when he was younger.

There had been a couple of other women since Jennifer had walked out on him. But he had never been entranced. Or captivated. Or enchanted.

Until now.

He wanted her—*her,* Tori Jones, in particular. Not just someone suitably attractive and well-bred, as Jennifer had been. Not just someone sophisticated, sexually exciting and discreet, which pretty much described the two women he'd dated after his marriage crashed and burned.

It came to him that he...he *liked* this woman. And that was new to him. He liked her quick wit, her wisdom and her big heart. He liked the passion in her voice when she talked about things she believed in.

He liked *her.* And suddenly it mattered all out of proportion that she might like him, too.

Was he losing it? He couldn't help but wonder. Was cracking under the strain—of the soured economy, the ?arlane House setbacks, his divorce, the scary changes son? Of the changes he'd decided he needed to make ?e and himself?

Strangely, right then, on his first date with Tori Jones, he didn't care if he just might be going over the edge. He was having a great time—having *fun,* of all things—and he didn't want it to end.

Is Connor finally able to admit his feelings to Tori,
and are they reciprocated?
Find out in McFARLANE'S PERFECT BRIDE
by USA TODAY bestselling author Christine Rimmer.
Available July 2010,
only from Silhouette Special Edition®.

Bestselling Harlequin Presents® author

Penny Jordan

brings you an exciting new trilogy…

Needed:
THE WORLD'S MOST
ELIGIBLE
BILLIONAIRES

Three penniless sisters:
how far will they go to save the ones they love?

Lizzie, Charley and Ruby refuse to drown in their debts.
And three of the richest, most ruthless men in the world
are about to enter their lives. Pure, proud but penniless,
how far will these sisters go to save the ones they love?

Look out for

Lizzie's story—**THE WEALTHY GREEK'S**
CONTRACT WIFE, July

Charley's story—**THE ITALIAN DUKE'S**
VIRGIN MISTRESS, August

Ruby's story—**MARRIAGE: TO CLAIM HIS TWIN**
September

www.eHarlequin.com

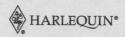
HARLEQUIN®

Showcase

LESLIE KELLY
Naturally Naughty

Wicked & Willing

On sale June 8

Reader favorites from the most talented voices in romance

Save $1.00 on the purchase of 1 or more Harlequin® Showcase books.

SAVE $1.00 on the purchase of 1 or more Harlequin® Showcase books.